RETURN TO SLEEPING BEAR

Enjoy your journey
to Sleeping Bear!

Mary K. Eastman

Readers are encouraged to go to www.MissionPoint-
Press.com to contact the author or to find information
on how to buy this book in bulk at a discounted rate.

Published by Mission Point Press
2554 Chandler Rd.
Traverse City, MI 49696
(231) 421-9513
www.MissionPointPress.com

ISBN: 978-1-943995-92-9
Library of Congress Control Number: 2018966783

Printed in the United States of America.

RETURN TO SLEEPING BEAR

MARY K. EASTMAN

MISSION POINT PRESS

In loving memory of my dad and mom,
Kenneth and Rose Eastman

You always believed in me and made
me believe in myself. Although you've
passed on, I still feel the warmth of
your love every day.

Love you and miss you,
Mary

BEGINNINGS

CHAPTER ONE

Bree frowned as she looked out the window and saw how hard it was raining. The drive would be slow, making it difficult to get to work on time. Grabbing her purse and jacket, she headed toward the door.

Normally Bree liked driving to work—it was a scenic route that wound its way around the north and west side of Crystal Lake. But the rain came down in torrents today, covering the windshield as fast as the wipers could swipe it away. She could barely see ten feet ahead.

As she came to a curve and neared Point Betsie Road, she brushed her thick, long strands of chocolate-brown hair behind her shoulders, keeping her eyes focused intently on the road.

"Oh shoot!" she cried out. Hitting the brakes and stopping the car, she just missed a woman running across the roadway. She honked at the stranger, making her stumble to the ground. Bree pulled over, jumped out, and stood in the rain, hollering to her. The woman slowly got up and took off running again, not looking back. Bree chased after her.

"Hey, lady! Are you crazy? You could've been killed!"

The woman hesitated a second, frantically looking left and right. Catching just a glimpse of the side of her face, Bree guessed she was in her mid-forties. Her drenched dress clung to her body. Bree waited, hoping she'd turn back and talk to her. Instead, she took off again, turning left and heading north, into the woods.

"I'm not going to hurt you!"

The woman kept running.

"Oh, forget it," she muttered, heading back to her car.

As Bree wiped the rain from her eyes, there was another flash of lightning. It lit the sky long enough to reveal the silhouette of a man standing twelve feet away by the roadside. He wore a navy waterproof jacket with the hood pulled close around his face, making it difficult to see his features. As quickly as he appeared, he vanished. The darkness cloaked him from her sight.

Bree ran to her car. Never before was she so glad to see her beat-up Camaro. Glancing around, she jumped in and locked the doors. Where had he gone? Was he watching or following? Had he been chasing that woman and gone after her again?

Fumbling nervously with the key, she started the car and took off, glancing frequently in her rearview mirror. Far behind her, she saw headlights. It was a welcome sight when the Lakeshore Bar came into view. She waited until the car behind her drove past to leave her vehicle and enter the bar. Inside, finally, she let out a sigh of relief. The familiar surroundings comforted her—pictures of storm-blustered ships and harbor-town mementos such as ship wheels and anchors adorned the walls. Warm light glowed on the polished bar.

"Well, look at what dregs the rain washed in," said Charlie, an off-duty police officer, sitting at the bar. Despite his diminishing amount of hair and the spare tire starting to develop around his midsection, he was considerably attractive.

"Where have you been?" asked Larry, the bar's owner. "You look awful."

"I love you too," Bree answered, tossing her purse on the bar. "You will not believe what just happened. On my way here, a woman ran out in front of me. I almost nailed her, but she kept running. I ran after her, called to her, but she wouldn't stop. She looked panicked, like she wasn't all there—seemed out of her head with fright or something..." Rambling on, she poured out everything that had happened.

When she finished, Charlie looked at her wide-eyed. "Don't tell me you've seen her?"

"Seen who?" Bree asked.

"People on that road claim they've seen the ghost of a woman who was lost in a boating accident a few years ago, just beyond Point Betsie."

"A ghost? Come on!"

Charlie turned to the owner of the bar. "Larry, do you mean to tell me you never told Bree about the ghost of Point Betsie?"

"Of course not," Larry said. "You know I don't believe that garbage."

"Well," Charlie continued, turning back to look at Bree, "If Larry won't tell you, I will. There was a family boating on Lake Michigan at night, and they got into some kind of trouble. No one knows exactly what happened, but those waters can be treacherous. The lighthouse warns people, but..." Charlie hesitated for effect. "Anyway, three of the bodies were recovered, but the woman's body was never found. Some people claim they've seen her running along the shoreline on stormy nights, looking for her husband and children."

"Really?" Bree asked. Her wet hair clung to her head, her brown eyes opening wide as she waited to hear more. "Is that true?" She turned toward Larry, who had his back to her. He was trying, but couldn't hold it in any longer. He burst into laughter, with Charlie joining in louder.

"He got you good this time, Bree," Larry said between chuckles. "I can't believe you fell for it."

Normally Bree took kidding well, but tonight was different. Her experience on the road had left her shaken.

"Stop it! This may be funny to you, but it's not funny to me! That woman was scared. I think a man was chasing her. I got in his way, but he could've done something to her or me. Who knows what he was up to, or capable of?"

"What man?" Charlie asked earnestly. "You didn't mention a man."

"When I turned to head back to my car, there was a man standing a few yards away."

"I'll call it in," Charlie said, picking up his cell phone.

"I don't know if that's necessary. The woman was running fast, and he looked like he'd given up. I'd never be able to identify him anyway. It was too dark, and his hood hid most of his face."

"You're probably right. I doubt if they'll find anything, but I'll have one of the guys take a drive out that way. It couldn't hurt." He quickly made the call, then returned his attention to his half-finished beer.

"I'm sorry, Bree," Larry said, running his fingers through his thick, slightly graying dark hair. "I guess it was mean to tease like that, but you made it so easy. Take a few minutes to change and pull yourself together. I owe you that much."

Larry felt guilty about laughing at Bree. What if she really had been in danger? Larry had owned the bar for fifteen years and felt protective of his waitresses; standing six feet three and weighing a solid 240 pounds, he didn't often have trouble.

Bree changed into dry clothes she kept there for moments like this, but was still stuck with wet, squeaky shoes.

Oh well, it could be worse, she thought.

Getting right to work and occupying herself with customers kept her mind off things.

"Fred, if you don't remove your hand from my hip right now, I'll remove it for you."

"Shoot, Bree, an old man like me doesn't get to enjoy too many thrills these days."

"You'll enjoy even less with a hand missing."

Larry smiled to himself. Bree had been good for business. The regulars didn't mind her feisty, sometimes sarcastic wit. They admired her spunk. She had a good sense of humor and put up with a lot, but knew where to set the limit. Her good looks didn't hurt any either, he had to admit. She had a slim figure, long lashes, and beautiful eyes that sparkled when she laughed.

"Come on, Bree," Charlie said, "sing us a song."

Although it was karaoke night, Bree didn't feel like singing. "No thanks, I have tables to wait on. Why don't you sing for us, Charlie? I bet you sing like a pretty little songbird."

"I would, but you know me. I don't want to break the girls' hearts. They'd all be fighting over me, but I'm not that kind of guy."

"Uh huh," she said. "Your nose is growing, Pinocchio."

"We want Bree," Charlie chanted, pounding on the table. "We want Bree," he kept chanting, and was soon joined by others. She looked helplessly at Larry, and with a wave he gave permission.

She took off her apron and told another waitress, Sheila, the song she wanted to sing. Even though they were complete opposites, they had become good friends. Sheila was in her early forties and liked to flirt with the male customers. Bree, twenty-two, didn't like to encourage the kind of attention that Sheila actively sought out.

Loving the spotlight, Sheila eagerly stepped up to the microphone. Her tight short black skirt attracted attention to the little wiggle in her walk. She wore black nylons and shoes, but had hair as fiery as her personality. Wearing a white blouse, as was required of all the waitresses, she left it unbuttoned enough to show a teasing amount of cleavage.

"Drum roll, please," Sheila commanded with enthusiasm. The customers obliged by banging on the tables. Sheila laughed, tossing her head back. "Ladies and gentlemen, I am pleased to bring you our very own Brianna Lynn Darby, singing 'Me and Bobby McGee'! Let's give it up." Stepping to the side, her bracelets jangled as she raised her hands to applaud.

Bree took the microphone and started singing with a mellow tone.

The song was an old rock song with a funky, bluesy beat. As the tempo picked up, Bree let the music take over and poured her heart into it.

She encouraged the listeners to sing along, and even walked over to Charlie, ruffling up what little hair he had. For the finale she went back to the stage, finishing with a vocal climax that brought her audience to their feet.

Everyone clapped and hooted, especially Charlie. "Encore, encore!" he shouted.

"You never get enough, do you Charlie?" Bree asked.

"No. I never do. That's my problem."

Charlie enjoyed giving Bree a tough time. Being a recently divorced police officer, he was in no hurry to go home. The people at the bar were a family of sorts.

By closing time, Bree was beat and couldn't wait to head home. Her own customers kept her so busy that she barely noticed the man sitting at the back table. He was at one of Sheila's tables, so she paid no notice, but he did. He knew that he wanted to get to know Bree better. Someday, he would know her a lot better.

CHAPTER TWO

Bree tossed and turned. Faceless images of the man and woman taunted her. What were two people doing in that desolate area on such a nasty night? Who were they?

Finally, she nodded off. Around seven, she woke in a panic, her heart racing. She couldn't remember the dream she'd been having. After another hour or two of trying to go back to sleep, Bree gave up and got groggily out of bed.

Her day was not starting well. Making coffee and toast, she stared out the window. The apartment she lived in was the second floor of an old farmhouse, and had a pleasant view. The grass and trees were green and had sprung to life. Hearing the birds outside made her glad winter was over.

Pouring herself another cup of coffee, she tried to forget what had happened the night before, but it was useless. Thoughts of the poor rain-drenched woman plagued her. After wrestling with the previous night's events over and over, she decided to go back and investigate.

Bree put on sweats and headed for Point Betsie. Slowing down at the curve where the woman had been, she shivered, recalling vividly the mysterious man in the woods. Hoping the woman was all right, she turned down the road to Point Betsie, parked her car at the dead end, and walked to the beach. A fog had settled over the water and wrapped itself around the lighthouse.

Walking along the beach and kicking at the heavy wet sand, Bree headed toward the lighthouse. Attached to it was a white two-story home with a red roof. Along the south side stood a row of tall, thin, scraggly Lombardy trees. The trees were lined up like soldiers and looked out of place in the otherwise-natural setting. She knew they served as a windbreak, but they were just plain ugly, almost as ugly as her mood.

Bree tried to shake the dismal way she was feeling. This was her favorite beach. Yet now, her focus was on the one thing she didn't like—those few scraggly trees.

Choosing a bench to sit on, she looked out over the lake for the longest time, listening to the waves rush up on the shore. Sitting there, she felt a loneliness enthrall her like never before. There was no explanation for it, but for reasons she couldn't fathom, she embraced it and didn't want to let it go.

Down the shore she spotted a friend of hers, Denver Whitebird, jogging. When he saw Bree, he waved and slowed to a walk. Bree smiled to herself. He certainly didn't look bad: a lean, well-toned body, gorgeous smile, and intense eyes that could hold you. Not a trace of winter fat.

A year ago, when she moved north near Crystal Lake, she had come to Point Betsie often and occasionally saw Denver jogging. They talked easily and openly, and soon became friends. Through the bitter, cold months of winter they seldom saw each other—a bump-in at the store here, a chance encounter in the same restaurant there. Now that it was spring and Bree was regularly running into him again, she began to realize how much she had missed him. The realization surprised her. He wasn't like any of the guys she'd previously dated.

"Hey, Bree. How are you doing?" Denver asked, bringing her back to reality.

"Fine, how about you?"

"Okay," he said, sitting down next to her. "Perfect weather for a run—not too hot. Not too cold."

"It's brisker than I like, but I don't mind."

He glanced at her as she stared wistfully at the lake. "You seem distracted. Are you okay?"

Bree hesitated for a moment, then proceeded to go over the previous night's events with him.

"Wow," he said. "That was quite a night. You must've been scared."

"You could say that."

"I understand why this would bother you, but is that the only thing on your mind? I've seen that troubled look you get when you think nobody's watching. You seem to be drawn here."

Bree squirmed uncomfortably. "It's beautiful here. You come here often yourself."

Denver laughed. "You have a good point."

Bree hesitated for a moment. "Actually, you're right. I do have a connection with this beach. I was two years old when I was abandoned here; I grew up in the suburbs of Detroit with the family that found and adopted me. Mom, Dad, and my brother Steven. I don't like using the word 'adopted' because it sounds cold. Mom and Dad have always loved me and they've been open about my adoption, but when it came to any details or actually discussing it, they avoided the issue. There were times I would throw tantrums, demanding they tell me. It would always upset Mom, so I tried to put it out of my mind."

"Wow, I didn't know you were adopted. Being abandoned like that must have been tough."

"I'm sure it was. Of course, I don't remember any of that now, but it still hurts knowing your birth mom didn't want you. On my 21st birthday, Mom handed me some newspaper clippings and a sheet of paper. On the paper were the words, 'Please take care of my little Brianna. I cannot give her the life she should have. You will find her among the rocks.' The note looked like it was scribbled in a hurry, and the spelling was poor. The boy that gave them the note said a woman paid him to bring it to them. They heard me crying and found me by those rocks just over there," she said, pointing.

Denver used his fingertip to blot away a tear from her cheek. Bree smiled shyly, trying to compose herself.

"It may seem crazy, but after reading that note, I knew I needed to make some decisions about my life. All I could think of was this place and moving up here. Mom and Dad understood and helped me get started."

"Are you hoping your mother will come looking for you someday and find you here?"

"I will admit that I do dream of meeting her; what she would be like and what we would talk about. It's not that I need another mom. I don't. It's just that I don't know anything about myself, who my ancestors are or anything. You have so much pride in your heritage. You're on the council, and active in everything going on with your people. I don't even know when my real birthday is. Can you imagine what it's like to want desperately to learn something about yourself, but there's nothing but dead ends?"

"No, I can't say that I can."

Bree hesitated a moment. "The note said she couldn't give me the kind of life I should have. I often wonder if she was poor, had a terminal illness, or just didn't want me."

"You may never have the answers to those questions. Can you accept that, or would you like to look for her?"

"I've thought about it, but I wouldn't know where to begin. This may sound crazy, but I believe in fate or some higher power guiding our destiny. If we're meant to find each other, we will."

"That's a good attitude to take."

They sat staring silently out at the water.

"It's just so beautiful," Bree said with a sigh. "I never get tired of it."

"There's an art shop in Harbor Springs that had a painting of this beach and lighthouse. It was done by a local artist and not too pricey, so I bought it."

"Really?" Bree asked. "I'd like to see it sometime."

"Do you have time now?"

"Yes, I've got lots of time before I have to get ready for work, but don't you want to finish your jog?"

"I can jog anytime. I don't get to talk to you often. My car is parked by Crystal Lake, about a mile from here, if you don't mind walking."

"Mine is right here. I might as well drive."

Denver gave her directions and they talked on the way. Bree liked that she felt comfortable with him, and that conversation was easy.

His house was a small three-bedroom ranch on a wooded lot, with vinyl siding, a stone chimney, and a wood deck the length of the front of the house. There was a glider and rocker on the porch, which added to the home's cozy, welcoming appeal.

Once inside, Denver went to get his grandmother. While waiting, Bree glanced around. Decorative plates of Chippewa warriors and women were arranged on shelves on the wall, and brightly colored Indian blankets draped the backs of the couches and chairs. Pictures of family also hung on the walls.

When they came in the room, Denver introduced them. Grandmother was a short, frail lady, but walked with a spirited pep in her step. Her hair, which was halfway down her back and mostly gray, was tucked behind her ears. She greeted Bree with a warm smile and offered to make coffee. Bree accepted.

"While you're getting the coffee ready, Grandmother," Denver said, "I'm going to show Bree my Point Betsie painting."

She nodded for them to go on.

"I hope you don't mind," Denver said. "Grandmother loves to have visitors and she doesn't get that many."

"I don't mind at all. From the things you've told me, I know I'll enjoy talking to her."

Denver led Bree to a back bedroom he used as an office. Over his desk hung a big corkboard covered with snapshots of family, friends, his boat, the fish they'd caught, and Lake Michigan. He had some models of ships, and on one wall was the big painting he'd told her about. In the right-hand corner of the painting was the lighthouse tower, a soft beam of light shining out over the lake. Water crashed against a breakwater and sprayed upward. The sun had sunk low, partially hiding behind clouds; splashes of orange streaked through the gray. Seagulls walked along the shore, and a child with her mother was looking for treasures in the sand.

Denver stood back and watched the expression on Bree's face.

"It's wonderful. It's so real and detailed; it makes me feel like I'm there."

"That's exactly how I felt. I love being on the lake. There's something about the wind, the rocking of the boat, the scenery... Even when I'm here in my office, when I look at that picture I can go there in my mind."

Bree looked at him thoughtfully. She shared his love for the water and understood how he felt. "It sure does take you there, doesn't it? It's beautiful."

Going back to the kitchen, they sat down to drink the coffee.

"Are you the one from the beach that Denver has spoken of?" Grandmother asked.

Bree wasn't sure how to answer the question. Having no idea if Denver had mentioned her or not, she looked to him for help.

"Yes, Bree is the one who moved here last summer."

"I see," Grandmother said, sitting back in her chair. She pursed her lips together and squinted her eyes, as if trying to piece a big mystery together. "Is there anyone special in your life, Bree?"

"Grandmother!" Denver said, then explained to Bree, "Grandmother isn't known for being subtle. She loves playing matchmaker. If you're not careful, she'll have us married before you walk out the door."

"I will not," Grandmother said, but not being easily deterred, she turned back to Bree. "Well, is there?"

She laughed as Denver shook his head and covered his face with his hands. "No, I don't have any commitments at this time."

Denver left the room to change. Bree and Grandmother chatted and were laughing together when he came back.

"I'm afraid to ask," Denver said as he sat down.

"Your grandmother was telling me about the time your sister

talked you into climbing a tree and tying a rope around a beehive. I can't believe she ran in the house after telling you to pull the rope."

"I can't either. I never finished getting the rope on the beehive because I got stung a couple times."

"He swelled up like a marshmallow," Grandmother said, puffing up her cheeks. Bree laughed.

"What else can you tell me about this guy?"

"Well, there is the time he went snipe hunting."

"What are snipes?"

Denver smiled, shaking his head. "They told me snipes were furry little animals, similar to squirrels and good to eat."

"His cousins told him they would beat the bushes, driving the snipes his way. He was out there for a long time," Grandmother said, laughing so hard she was wiping tears from her eyes. "He took a brown paper bag, just like they told him, and hollered, 'Here snipe, here snipe.' He would not give up, so I made them tell him the truth—a snipe is a bird. I was proud of my brave little hunter."

"That's hilarious."

"I didn't think so at the time."

"He wouldn't talk to us at all the next day."

"Did you teach him how to fish, too?"

"Oh no," Denver said. "She taught me a lot, but not how to fish. You couldn't bring yourself to put a hook through a live worm, could you, Grandmother?"

"No, not at all. There's nothing wrong with it, but I could never do it. I always felt bad for the poor wriggling worm."

After chatting a while longer, Bree got up to say goodbye. "It was nice meeting you, Mrs. Whitebird."

"Call me Grandmother, most people do." Standing up, she smiled and reached for Bree's hand to give it a pat, but when they touched, her face paled.

"Ohhh," she said, pulling her hand away. Suddenly dizzy, she leaned on a chair to steady herself.

"Are you okay?" Bree asked, alarmed.

Grandmother's hands shook. "I'm okay. I'm fine—just need to sit down."

Denver helped her to a chair.

"I'll be fine. It's just another dizzy spell. You two go on."

Bree could see Denver's concern. "We can stay. I've got a lot of time before I have to be at work."

Grandmother insisted, so they agreed to go.

"I'll be right back, Grandmother. As soon as I get my jeep."

Bree drove Denver to the scenic turnout at Crystal Lake, where he was parked.

"What do you think is wrong with Grandmother?" Bree asked.

"I'm not sure. She's been having these dizzy spells for a while, and I can't convince her to see a doctor. She gets mad if anyone makes a fuss over her."

"I hope she'll be all right."

"Me, too. Well, I guess I'd better head back," he said, getting out of the car.

"Call me tomorrow to let me know how she's doing."

"I will," he said, and hurried off.

CHAPTER THREE

Late the next morning, Denver called to give Bree an update. Grandmother was doing fine and had told Denver to go find something to do. She didn't want him hovering over her.

"Since she booted me out of the house, how would you like to go for a boat ride with me this afternoon?"

Bree smiled, unable to think of anything she would enjoy more. "I'd love to."

"I'll pick you up at noon."

"That sounds good, but what about dinner? If we're going to be out there for a while, I could pick something up at the deli for us."

"Sure. That would be great."

They said goodbye and Bree headed to the deli, picking up potato salad, cold cuts, cheese, and some rolls to make submarine sandwiches. After getting everything she needed, she headed home, smiling.

Back at the apartment, Bree got right to work. Mrs. Anderson, who lived downstairs, was a little deaf, so Bree could crank the music up and nobody complained.

While quickly touching up the place, she belted out the words to her favorite songs and danced the vacuum cleaner around the living room. Next, she made the subs and wrapped them in baggies. In a small blue cooler she placed some ice packs, the subs, salad, and grapes.

Seeing some of the chocolate-chip cookies she'd made a couple days ago, Bree wondered if she should bring them too. Or would that be overdoing it? He might expect the royal treatment all the time. She wanted lunch to be nice, but not to look like she was trying too hard. *What the heck*, in went the cookies.

Realizing she was already assuming, or hoping, there would be a second date, she smiled to herself. Countless times her first dates turned out to be disasters, but she and Denver were good friends; she couldn't imagine them not getting along. But then again, he'd never said this was a date. He just asked her to go for a boat ride. Maybe that was all it was meant to be in his eyes—just two friends enjoying a boat ride together. Bree frowned as she thought about it. Denver wasn't currently involved with anyone, yet for all the times they'd talked he never showed interest in anything more than a friendship between them. Maybe she wasn't his type, and friends was all they would ever be.

Oh well, she thought, *I'll find out his intentions, or lack of them, soon enough.*

She put on a mauve T-shirt and jeans, pulling her hair up in a ponytail so it wouldn't get tangled from the wind. She looked at the perfume bottle sitting on the dresser. *Why not?* She grabbed it and dabbed a little behind her ears, then put on makeup.

Just before noon the doorbell rang. Bree ran to answer it.

"I'm almost ready," she said, letting him in.

"Take your time. I'm not in a hurry," he answered, looking around. "You have a nice apartment. I take it you like plants."

"How did you guess? Did my miniature jungle give it away?"

"That might have been it," he said as he touched the tips of a healthy-sized fern up on a pedestal.

"That's Wilbur," she said.

"Wilbur? You name your plants?"

"Of course. I have to call them something when I talk to them."

"You talk to your plants?"

"Yes. They say it's good for them. See that plant over there with the purple flowers?" she asked, pointing down the hall. "That's Abigail. She's a bougainvillea."

"I hope I'm not going to have to learn all their names."

"No," she said, laughing. "They're my buddies and keep me company. This place may not be much, but it's home."

It was a tiny, modest apartment, filled with furniture her parents had given her. When Bree moved out, she'd inherited the old sofa set they had in the basement. The small, but growing, collection of flowering plants and ferns gave the apartment her personal touch.

"Could you grab my blue jacket out of the closet?"

"Sure," he said. When he got to the closet he read aloud the caption from the poster on the door. "Feel the rush. Dare to dream." The picture was of people whitewater-rafting down a foaming, raging river. Water was crashing over the front of the raft. "Are you the adventurous type?"

Bree stood next to Denver and looked at the poster. "Actually, it was my brother's poster. I always loved it. When he went away to college, he gave it to me."

"That was nice. I take it you two are close?"

"We are now, but we fought a lot when we were younger. He had the spotlight to himself until I came along. At times he could be mean, but I suppose that's just a brother thing. I'm so glad," she said, changing the subject, "that your grandmother is okay."

"She's doing well," he said slowly, his voice taking on a serious tone. "It's you she was worried about. I don't know what you believe in, and you may think that I've gone off the deep end, but...I need to talk to you about something."

"What is it?"

"You're in danger and must be careful of who you trust."

"What do you mean? You're starting to scare me."

"I don't want to scare you," he answered earnestly, "but if it makes you more careful, that's good. You do act impulsively at times."

"What makes you think I'm in danger? Who would want to hurt me?"

"I don't know who, but how I know I can tell you. No, I don't have any special powers or receive visions, or anything like that," he said, cynicism showing in his voice. "But Grandmother has the gift. Yesterday when she touched your hand she saw a vision. Some call it ESP. Call it whatever you want, but she urged me to warn you."

Bree was stunned and didn't know what to say. She had heard of people with a gift like that and knew Denver wouldn't lie to her, but she wasn't ready to accept the possibility of danger.

"If she has this special ability, why haven't you mentioned it to me before?"

"Most people will brush off anything that can't be explained, so it's not something I mention to just anybody. But I do know her gift is real. My dad had a drinking problem when I was growing up; occasionally he would get out of control. There was one time when he went into a rage. I don't remember what set him off, but he was throwing things at the wall and yelling. I had never seen him like that before. We were all scared, and even though no one called her, Grandmother showed up at the door and took us kids home with her for the night. Another time she called my mom, wanting to know if everyone was okay. She was frantic and called all our other close relatives too. That night we were told her sister had been killed in a car accident—it happened around the same time she started calling everyone. She knew something was wrong before anyone was notified."

"Wow," Bree answered, rubbing her arms. "I've got goosebumps just thinking about it."

"I don't mean to scare you, Bree, but I had to tell you. If I didn't and something bad happened to you, I would never forgive myself."

"You're a good friend," said Bree, trying to smile. "I promise I'll be careful."

Denver and Bree took the lunch she had prepared down the stairs and loaded it into his jeep. "I love jeeps," Bree said, glad to have a distraction from their previous conversation. She settled comfortably into the seat. It wasn't even a year old, definitely nicer than her beat-up Camaro. She liked her car, but it was getting old and running rough lately. She turned on the radio, enjoying the music.

Denver could tell that Bree was having a fun time. She adjusted the seat and then the radio to suit her. "You don't mind, do you?"

"No, go right ahead," Denver answered, smiling at the way she made herself right at home.

"I bet it handles nice."

"Would you like to drive it?"

"You're kidding. I'd love to!"

"Let's switch, then."

Bree didn't hesitate. After running around the front of the jeep and getting in, she moved the seat forward and adjusted the mirrors. She was grinning as she grabbed the shifter and pulled out. As she got familiar with the vehicle she increased speed, taking the curves at an impressive pace, wind wildly blowing her hair. "This is great," she said, picking up more speed on the straightaway.

Denver grabbed the dash, pretending to fear for his life.

Bree laughed and reached to swat him.

"You didn't warn me you had a lead foot."

"It does get heavy at times," she admitted. "My dad's a mechanical engineer and loves fast vehicles. I guess it might have rubbed off on me."

"You think?"

When they reached the marina, Bree hesitated to get out. "You can go on alone," she said, teasing him. "I'll just cruise around in this for a while."

"I don't think so," he answered. "I don't trust you. You wouldn't come back."

"That's a possibility, but eventually I'd get low on gas. I'd come back then."

As they walked down the dock, Bree warned him. "First I get to drive your jeep and now I get a boat ride. You're going to spoil me."

"Nothing wrong with that," he answered, smiling.

Denver boarded his boat, the Nighthawk, and held out his hand to help Bree step down from the dock. A few years ago, he had bought a used Boston Whaler for recreational fishing and personal use, complete with a head and a small cuddy. On deck, there was some walking space and a cushioned cooler to sit on. There was a captain's chair and another chair next to it. Denver sat in one of them, Bree in the other, as he steered the Nighthawk out of the marina. The town of Frankfort slowly disappeared behind them; out ahead stretched nothing but sapphire-blue water meeting the azure sky. Beautiful. Bree could smell the moist, clean air and feel the gentle breeze blowing on her skin. She carefully made her way on the walkaround to the bow, where she knelt. Denver picked up speed, and the front of the boat slapping the waves sent a spray of water right into Bree's face. She shrieked.

"That wasn't very nice," she said, scolding.

Denver was grinning wickedly. "Whoever said I was nice?"

"Certainly not me," she said, then ordered him to go faster.

Denver obeyed her command and Bree grabbed the rail to steady herself. She loved the wind in her face and the gentle spray of the water.

Bree finally turned around, facing the captain of the vessel. He looked so handsome there at the wheel. The wind was blowing his shoulder-length hair. She crossed her legs and stretched her arms out on the rail. He had high cheekbones, thin lips, and bottomless brown eyes; his skin was a deepened bronze. She definitely found him attractive, but felt the need to conceal the intensity of her attraction, at least for now. That was one of the things that often got Bree into trouble; she would dive into relationships, instinctively going with her emotions and getting involved too soon, mistaking pure physical attraction for love. She was going to have to watch herself this time.

What Bree was unaware of was that Denver had been studying her as much as she had been studying him. Her lips had just enough fullness to them to be enticing. Her thick, brown curls bounced in her ponytail; wisps of hair that had escaped blew around her face, framing it. He liked her long, thin legs and slender body. Denver couldn't seem to get her out of his mind lately. He liked everything about her. Sometimes she had the spirit and innocence of a child, enjoying life to the fullest. Yet, at other times she seemed far wiser than her years.

After heading north for a half hour, Denver stopped the Nighthawk so they could eat their dinner. Neither one of them had had any lunch, so eating early sounded great. They went down into the cabin and fixed their plates. Denver got out two glasses and a bottle of wine.

"Fine wine with my sub sandwiches? This is another first to add to my list for the day. You don't need the wine to help choke down my store-bought specials, do you?"

Denver laughed. "Actually, I like sandwiches and the deli bread is delicious. As for the wine—it's always appropriate for special occasions and pretty ladies," he said, raising his glass.

Unaccustomed to hearing things like that from Denver, she blushed. "Are you trying to flatter me? You said earlier that I shouldn't trust anyone. Should I trust you?"

"Never," he answered, grinning.

They took their time eating, enjoying the gentle rocking of the boat. "Well," he finally said, "we better get moving if we're going to get there."

"Get where? You never told me where we were going."

"I thought I'd take you to South Manitou Island. You have heard the legend about the islands, haven't you?"

"Yes, I have, but it's been a while. I know this legend is real, unlike the ones Charlie tells. I'd like to hear it again."

He began to tell the story. "Long ago near the shores of Wisconsin, there were two cubs playing in the woods, near their mother. They were wrestling around when they heard strange sounds. They wrinkled their noses as they smelled something unfamiliar. Flocks of birds were frantically flying overhead, squawking their warnings. Rabbits, squirrels, and other animals were running wildly past them. The mother bear saw the smoke in the sky and heard the crackling sounds. She pushed her cubs and drove them away from the fire that was getting closer each minute. Being trapped on the Lake Michigan shore, they had no place to run. The mother bear drove her cubs into the water to escape the fire. They swam and swam in an eastward direction, growing more tired as they went. On through the night they continued. As the winds picked up and the waves grew larger, the mother bear urged her cubs to continue following her. Occasionally they lost sight of her. Finally reaching the eastern shore of Lake Michigan, the mother bear climbed to the top of a dune to wait for her cubs. She kept waiting for them and would not leave, but the cubs had grown too tired to go further and they drowned. The mourning mother bear would not leave, still hoping and watching. When she finally died, Great Spirit Manitou marked her place of rest with a dune that today is called Sleeping Bear and raised two islands, North and South Manitou, in honor of her brave cubs."

Bree sat silently, thinking about the mother bear grieving for her lost cubs. It made her sad, but she was also feeling relaxed. She didn't know if it was his soothing voice, the wine, or the gentle rocking of the waves, but she did know she was feeling mellow and serene.

As they approached South Manitou Island, Bree was struck with awe. It was gorgeous. The banks were low and forested when you looked toward the east side of the island, but as you looked toward the west the banks steadily rose. On the west side of the island, gleaming dunes rose high above the water. At the top of the dunes, a few trees were scattered here and there, where they managed to survive the blowing sands. The white sands of the dunes dropped steeply to the aqua waters of Lake Michigan—the water was several shades of blue, the hue deepening further out from shore. It went from light azure-greens to a deep, dark oceanic blue. The blend of colors pleased the eye.

Not far from the shoreline, Bree spotted the shipwreck of the Morazan. It was an old steel ship that had run aground years ago. Each year it sank a little further below the surface, but much of it could still be seen.

Denver brought the boat around the southeast corner of the

island, where the lighthouse was located. As he came around the corner and into the east bay, other buildings came into view.

The island was a national park where tourists could camp and go backpacking. Families had once lived on South Manitou, but after it became a national park no one was allowed to buy land or move to the island. Now it was uninhabited, except for the park rangers that lived there seasonally.

"It's beautiful," Bree said, looking at the passing shoreline.

"It's great here. Until Memorial Day weekend comes, you don't see many people, so I always feel like I have the island to myself. This sheltered bay on the east side is the safest area to dock."

Denver docked the boat and helped Bree out. He then pushed out to drop anchor and wade to shore, as was required by the park. They walked along the cement walkway past the houses, information center, and the lighthouse. Outside the old preserved buildings were wagons, plows, and other antique farm equipment on display for visitors to the island. The walkway changed to wood, and then into a dirt path.

"If you're up for it, I thought we could walk to the west side of the island and see the cedar trees and the dunes," said Denver.

"That would be great."

"It's around three miles to get there. It gets hilly at the end, and then we have to walk back."

"No problem. I think I can handle it. If not, you'll have to carry me."

Denver laughed. They walked along some trails, enjoying the scenery. The trail started to gradually wind upward when they reached the virgin white-cedar forest.

"Wow," Bree said, looking up at the gnarled gray-white cedars. "They're huge."

A posted sign gave possible explanations for why this group of cedars escaped the lumberman's ax. This stand was the furthest distance from East Bay, where the lumber was loaded onto ships. Also, the sand embedded in the bark would have been hard on their saws.

Bree and Denver continued up the trail. Bree had to stop now and then to catch her breath. It climbed steadily upward through the cedar forest. When her footing slipped, Denver reached out to steady her. Near the top, the trees were sparse. Bree could see the top of the dunes. Breathing in the fresh, breezy air, she knew that Lake Michigan had to be on the other side. They were finally there.

Bree made her way to the top and stood, looking down with disappointment at what she saw. Before her was a little dip and another looming dune. The two of them walked on. When they got to the top there was yet another dip and climb, but this one wasn't as big.

When they reached the top, Lake Michigan spread out before them. It was a welcome sight for Bree. The sun had begun its descent and was halfway down toward the horizon. They sat at the top looking out at the lake and sky. The sunlight glistened on the water. The breeze felt refreshing, and the dunes dropped steeply before them. The combination of the steep drop and the rocks mixed in with the sand made a fast descent treacherous. They settled on sitting and enjoying the view.

Denver rested his hand on Bree's leg. She tried ignoring the sensations going through her, stimulated just from the touch of his hand. Was it an innocent gesture, or was he attracted to her? Their conversation stayed casual, so Bree wasn't sure.

"Let's go," Denver said at length, getting up and extending his hand. "I have one more place I want to show you."

They trudged along until they reached a sand bowl.

"I always liked to run down the dunes as a kid," Denver said. "It's been a while since I've done it."

"No time like the present," Bree responded as she started down the hill. She went full speed, gravity making her go faster than she normally could. Her arms were flailing wildly at her sides. The strides down were so big it was almost as if she were gliding downhill. Bree was shouting and laughing at the reckless feeling of being out of control. Her legs could not keep up with her body any longer, and she unwillingly lunged forward and started tumbling down. Denver was right on her heels. Not being able to stop, he took a leaping dive over her. Moments later they were lying on the sand near each other, laughing and trying to get their breath back.

Denver recovered quickly. Crawling next to Bree, he raised his body up to lean on his elbow. He was looking down at Bree. Her face was flushed from the run downhill, and her eyes danced with laughter. He stretched his right leg over Bree's leg. Bree had her arms stretched over her head. He reached up to touch Bree's arm and let his hand and eyes travel slowly, ever so slowly downward, gently following the soft contours of her body. He rested his hand on her waist.

"What are you doing?" Bree questioned in a soft, meek voice.

He looked up. Their eyes locked as they looked at each other for what seemed like an eternity. In his eyes, Bree saw a longing and hunger that made her feel weak. He had never looked at her like that before.

"I'm sorry," he said, looking down at his hand like he was willing it to move. But, like a disobedient child, it refused to obey. He looked back into her eyes. "Ever since I watched you out on the bow of the boat, I've had this overwhelming urge to just touch you. I haven't been able to shake it."

Bree took in the words he was saying. Could it be that the feelings she was beginning to have about him were not unrequited? She turned to liquid beneath his touch. Her breathing was heavy—how much from the run and how much from the sensations pulsating through her body, she wasn't sure. But she couldn't fight it any longer.

"What took you so long?" Bree questioned as she pulled Denver's face down to her and kissed him with a driving hunger. She wrapped her legs around his, pulling his body on top of hers. Their kiss was full of passion, and Bree drank in the tenderness and emotion they were mutually feeling. She knew it was crazy to get so carried away so soon, but she didn't care.

Reason finally came back to her. What was she doing? The last serious relationship she had been in was disastrous. Her boyfriend turned out to be very possessive and controlling. His personality had changed so slowly that she hadn't even realized how much he manipulated and controlled her life. By the time she was aware of it, it was hard to break it off. She'd made a promise to herself to never rush into anything again—to take things slow—and here she was, jumping right in.

"I'm sorry, Denver," she said, pulling away. "We need to slow down. Things are moving too fast."

"No, Bree. I'm the one that should be apologizing. I was out of line. That wasn't the reason I brought you out here."

"Why *did* you bring me out here?"

"I guess I just wanted to spend some time with you, to get to know you better. I've wanted to ask you out, but we've been such good friends, I didn't know what you would think about it. This was a way to be with you until I worked up some courage."

Bree laughed. "I've been wondering myself how you felt. I guess we're both a couple of chickens. Maybe we should get up and get moving before things get out of hand again. It's going to be dark soon."

Denver gave her a quick kiss and extended his hand to help her up. Together they started their climb back up the sand bowl.

"Did you know that they actually have warning signs in some places that climbing dunes can be hazardous to your health?"

"Oh great, now you tell me."

"I didn't think it would be a problem," he said, while grinning and wrapping an arm around her. "You look pretty healthy to me."

They started their long trek back—climbing up and down the dunes, then descending back through the cedar forest. As they continued their long walk they talked about anything and everything that came to their minds.

"My ancestors, the Chippewa, would on rare occasions visit this island," Denver said, "but they wouldn't live here."

"Why is that?"

"A long time ago an entire camp was mysteriously wiped out while they were sleeping. My ancestors believed evil spirits lived on the island and were responsible for what happened. No one would live here after that."

"That's hard to imagine when you look at this place."

When Denver got the boat back to the dock, he helped her climb back on. Darkness was settling on the water as the sun said its final goodbye. Bree sat in the seat next to Denver. The moon shone its white orb of light, casting a soft, glowing path on the water that led directly to them. Bree sighed. It was exquisite.

Denver drove Bree home and helped her carry her cooler up to her apartment. They stood at the door to say goodbye.

"Thank you for everything," Bree said. "It's been a while since I've had so much fun."

"I've enjoyed myself, too," Denver answered. Then he grinned suggestively. "It doesn't have to end, you know."

Bree laughed. "As much as I hate to say it, yes, it does." They said goodnight and Bree went inside, plopping herself down on her bed and looking dreamily up at the ceiling. It had been a wonderful day.

CHAPTER FOUR

Bree and Denver started spending more and more time together, sometimes going for a boat ride, a walk along the beach, or just hanging out and talking for hours.

The Wednesday before Memorial Day weekend was Bree's day off and Denver took it off, too, so he could spend the whole day with her.

When he arrived, he announced that he was taking her somewhere special.

"Really?" she asked, intrigued. "Where?"

"It's a surprise."

"Well, you have to tell me. I won't know what to wear or if I should dress up or not."

He looked her over, noticing her snug-fitting jeans and Michigan T-shirt. Smiling, he told her she looked perfect.

"Mmmm," she said, stepping in close and wrapping her arms over his shoulders. "If you keep saying things like that and looking at me that way, we just might not make it anywhere."

He pulled her in close. "Don't tempt me. You're making staying here sound real good, but I'd be wasting the tickets I bought. It's up to you."

"Tickets, you say. Hmmm," she said, her curiosity mounting. "Okay. You *have* to tell me. Where are we going?"

"You'll see. We should leave soon because we have to drive over to Traverse City. Oh, and I recommend you wear tennis shoes. And bring a jacket just in case."

She grabbed her tennis shoes and started to put them on. Then she got her jacket out of the closet. "I have to wear tennis shoes," she said, thinking. "On the way, you're not going to make me run up and down dunes again, are you?"

"No, not tonight," he said, laughing, "but I do remember that was a lot of fun. We'll have to do it again sometime."

"I agree," she said, remembering vividly how it felt when he'd run his hand down the length of her body. Staying was a temptation, but what did he have in store for her tonight? Her mind raced with the different possibilities as they walked to Denver's jeep and got in.

"Let me guess," she said, "We're going to a concert on the beach. It can get chilly at night by the water; that's why I need the jacket."

"No. As far as I know, there aren't any concerts in Traverse City tonight, but there should be plenty of bands playing this weekend with the holiday coming up."

"Oh! The concert isn't in Traverse City. Before we go to Traverse City, we're going to stop at the Interlochen Arts Academy. They might be having a concert tonight because it's the end of the school year."

Denver laughed. "You aren't very good at dealing with surprises, are you?"

"No," she said, grimacing. "I'm very bad at it."

"Well, it's not Interlochen."

They drove awhile, casually talking before she had another idea. With apprehension, she asked, "You do know I'm squeamish about heights, don't you? We're not zip-lining or jumping out of a plane, are we?"

Denver burst into laughter. "No, I didn't know you don't like heights. I would never try to get you to do something like that without asking you first. I think you have to be mentally prepared to jump out of a plane. I'd have to be, anyways."

"Me too. The preparation would have to include knocking me unconscious."

"You're one crazy lady," he said, laughing and shaking his head.

They drove on, talking about other things until they came to a big sign for a cherry orchard.

"That's it!" Bree said, slapping her leg. "You wanted me to wear tennis shoes because you're taking me to one of those wine tasting events. In case I get smashed, you don't want me tripping and falling on my face!"

"Ahhhhh! You're worse than a kid!" Denver exclaimed, but the smile on his face gave away his enjoyment.

After getting to Traverse City, Denver asked Bree to close her eyes.

"Why?"

"We're almost there."

Bree closed her eyes. "Can I peek?"

"No!"

After they drove a mile, then turned left, he had her open her eyes.

She looked around. "I can't believe it!" she said in mock surprise. "A parking lot. I've never been to one of those before."

He playfully swatted her shoulder. "Look over there," he said, pointing to a sign.

"Oh!" Bree said, genuinely excited. "We're going on the Manitou! I've always wanted to go sailing, but never have! Awesome!"

She reached over and gave him a kiss, then they got out and walked across the street to where the boat was docked. They checked in to get their tickets, then sat on the bench waiting and chatting with the other passengers who were arriving.

When it was time, everyone was given a welcoming speech before they boarded the ship. Denver and Bree picked a spot to sit in the front part of the schooner. The sails had been lowered when the previous group came in, so a motor was used to get them away from shore.

Once they were in open water, it was announced that they needed ten volunteers for each side to help hoist the main sail. Denver and Bree looked at each other and quickly got up to assist. Instructions were given for the commands.

Bree and Denver's group stood on the same side of the rope as instructed and picked it up when told to. When everyone was ready, the young crew member leading their group hollered, "Ready on the peak!"

The crew member for the other group hollered, "Ready on the throat!"

Next, the command was given to "haul away!"

Everyone pulled on the rope, hand over hand, passing it back to the person behind them. It started out slowly, but only for a second. The speed quickly increased and everyone was working hard. Bree was surprised at how fast they were pulling the rope and started laughing, but somehow managed to keep up.

Next, they were told to hold the line and then to drop the line.

When they looked up they could see the main sail raised, but the job wasn't even close to being done. The crew expertly and quickly moved around working the ropes and gave others a chance to help with the other sails.

"That was fun!" Bree said, as they watched the crew and passengers.

"I knew you would enjoy this."

Soon they were sailing out in Grand Traverse Bay!

As a band was setting up, the anchor was lowered.

"What band is playing?" Bree asked, grinning. "I was at least partly right about the concert."

"They're a local band called Song of the Lakes. Most of their songs are about the Great Lakes and the salty seas. They play folk music with an Irish flavor to their sound. You're gonna love it."

"I think you're right. I see guitars, a mandolin, and a flute."

The band introduced themselves and joked around a bit before their first song. The percussion instruments provided a toe-tappin', hand-clappin' beat. Throughout their performances they occasionally pulled out other instruments such as a bodhran, guiro, or maracas. The guitarists plucked out beautiful melodies and the flutist provided everything from the hollow sound of the wind to a chirping-type sound reminiscent of birds before a storm. They had the passengers captivated.

During a short break, the crew passed out a picnic lunch for everyone consisting of a wrap with a deliciously tangy sauce, a pasta salad, and for dessert—a big chocolate-chunk cookie. Denver bought them both a glass of wine from the cash bar.

While the passengers were enjoying their meal, the band started playing again; but before they did, they explained that the next few songs were inspired by a story written back in 1941 by Holling Clancy Holling. The story told of a boy long ago who lived in Nipigon, north of Lake Superior. During the long winter months, he carved out of wood an Indian man in a canoe and on the bottom carved the words "Please put me back in the water. I am Paddle to the Sea."

When spring came, he took Paddle to the Sea to a hill and set him in the snow. The Sun Spirit set him free and he rushed down the hill to Lake Superior. The songs tell of Paddle's adventures on his way through the Great Lakes to the salt waters.

While absorbed in the stories told in song, Bree leaned against Denver, putting her head on his shoulder as he wrapped his arm around her. They were completely immersed in the experience.

And if this weren't enough: the sky—not wanting to be out-done—decided to put on its own show. Early in the afternoon the day had been overcast, but the wind gently blew the dark clouds northward, pushing them out of the way to display harmless, puffy white clouds. Directly above and to the south, the sky was a clear pale blue. The sun was hiding behind the white curtain, waiting to present itself. It dropped just enough to only reveal the bottom part of its yellow orb, looking like a basketball stuck in a net. A bright disk of light reflected down on the water directly below. The sun continued to drop, releasing itself from the net of clouds and breaking free. The sky around the yellow orb burst into a brilliant apricot canvas. The small disk of light lengthened and stretched across the water like a kite tail.

Beautiful.

The Manitou was on its way back to the dock. The sails were lowered, the band packed up, and the sun was settling behind the hills and trees.

The passengers disembarked and Denver and Bree headed back to the jeep.

"That was a truly amazing evening. Everything was perfect: the boat, the music, the meal...and that beautiful sunset."

"Yes, it was amazing. They actually call that a false sunset," Denver said, "because it's setting behind the hills and trees. Sometimes people will watch a false sunset and then hurry to Lake Michigan and watch it set again—on the water. We were too slow. By the time we get there, the moon will be out."

"The night sky can be breathtaking too."

"I agree," Denver said. "On our way back, we can stop and see the moon on the water if you want."

"That would be great."

When they arrived at the beach on Lake Michigan, they got out and walked along the shoreline. The moon was shining above, blazing a quicksilver path on the water. The cool breeze felt good.

"We even have a full moon," Bree said. "Look how it's constantly changing with those clouds passing in front of it. Sometimes the moon's a big, bright ball and sometimes it has wispy clouds partially hiding it."

"The sky never gets boring because it's never the same."

They continued walking, holding hands. "Oh," Denver said, "I almost forgot. Grandmother and I would like to invite you to our family's Memorial Day picnic on Monday. It's at my house. Would you like to come?"

"That sounds great. Larry's giving me that day off because I'm working long hours on Friday, Saturday, and Sunday for the holiday crowd. Who's going to be there?"

"Just my sisters and their families, Grandmother of course, my parents and my aunts, uncles, and cousins. I volunteered to have it at my house this year to make it easier for Grandmother. If she gets tired, she can go inside and rest."

"So," Bree said, turning to look at him. "I'll be meeting your whole family this weekend."

"Does that make you nervous?"

"Just a little. Do you always bring your dates to family gatherings?" she asked, kidding him.

"Bree, I think you know that you're more to me than just another date. I can't label what I'm feeling, but I do know that I can't stop thinking about you, and I definitely don't want to spend my holiday without you."

The breeze gently played with her hair, blowing it away from her face. She smiled at him. "This day has been wonderful. The ride on the schooner, the music and sunset—everything. It's been perfect. Thank you," she said, and slowly gave him a tantalizing kiss, moving her body next to his, needing and wanting that connection. "I think we should head back to my apartment," she said in a soft, seductive voice.

Catching her meaning, he agreed. "I'll race you to the jeep."

They ran, laughing, to the jeep and when they got to her apartment they ran up the steps. Barely having time to get her shoes off, Denver swooped her up in his arms, carrying her to the bedroom.

The night was magical and full of surprises.

When Monday, the morning of the Memorial Day picnic, came, Bree eagerly started preparations. She made a fruit bowl and a blueberry cream cheese pie. Then she took a shower, getting herself ready. After changing her mind several times, she decided on a cream-colored T-shirt and a pair of shorts. She pulled her hair up in a ponytail. The picnic didn't start until two o'clock, and she arrived a few minutes early.

Grandmother was glad to see her and put her to work. Bree met everyone as they came in, trying to remember their names and hoping to make a good impression.

Some salads and desserts were brought. Denver's Aunt Leah brought a big bowl of corn soup, and Grandmother baked her traditional fry bread.

Denver got stuck at the grill cooking hamburgers and hot dogs. Everyone made Bree feel at home, and of course enjoyed teasing Denver.

Denver's cousin, John, sat next to Bree at the picnic table and hollered to him: "Don't worry, Denver, I'll take care of your friend here. Take your time." He winked at Bree, letting her know he was kidding.

"I think she was taking care of herself just fine," Denver answered back, laughing. After everyone was done eating and the food was cleared away, a game of volleyball was organized. Denver and Bree were put on opposite teams. It seemed to be a good-natured family joke to try to keep them apart.

When it started to get dark and the fire was started, Denver quickly sat next to Bree before anyone else could. He made it clear to everyone that he was not moving.

Hot dogs and marshmallows were roasted over the fire. Denver's little nieces were curious about the new visitor and fired questions at her.

"Are you Denver's girlfriend?"

"How long have you been going together?"

"Are your ears pierced?"

"Are you two going to get married?"

Bree kidded with the girls by giving them silly answers that made them giggle.

Then they turned on Denver. "Uncle Denver, who do you like better? Bree or Rose?"

Bree heard a few snickers and felt a tension in the air as they waited to see how Denver would handle the question.

"Girls," Denver's sister Terri intervened. "It's not polite to ask too many questions."

"Rose?" Bree asked, turning to Denver. "Who is Rose?"

"Rose is just an old girlfriend," he answered. "We broke up almost a year ago."

"A year ago, and the girls still talk about her? She must have made quite an impression on them."

Denver laughed, but there was an edge to his voice. "Rose has a way of making an impression on everyone she meets."

Bree thought about it for a moment, trying to picture what Rose might be like. She'd had boyfriends before and they meant nothing to her now, so why was she jealous of this Rose?

Denver seemed to be reading her mind. "I'm the one who decided to break up. She doesn't mean anything to me anymore."

Bree nodded and eventually put Rose out of mind as Denver snuggled up closer and put his arm around her. "I was beginning to think I would never get to spend any time with you," he said.

"I'm glad that you did."

Everyone encouraged Hannah, one of Denver's cousins, to play her guitar. She got it out and began to strum and sing songs. Her voice was soft and melodic, floating on the air. The fire crackled along with the music and the flames danced. A night breeze gently blew Hannah's beautiful long dark hair. The smaller children drifted off to sleep. The older children and the adults enjoyed the music for another hour or two before starting to disperse and go home.

Bree talked a while to Denver's parents before they left. She got busy right away helping Grandmother and Denver clean up in the kitchen.

After a few minutes, Grandmother mentioned wanting to talk to Bree alone.

"Grandmother," Denver said, "I don't think..."

"It's okay," Bree said. "I want to hear what she has to say."

Denver looked helplessly at the two of them before walking away. "I guess I'm outnumbered," he said, muttering to himself.

Grandmother wiped her hands off on the dish towel before beginning. "Bree," she said slowly, "I know Denver has told you of my vision, but I wanted to speak to you myself. I think of you as if you were one of my own grandchildren. I would not want to see you get hurt. This thing I see, it has no face. I cannot see its face," she said, frowning. "But it seeks to harm you. It's cold, vicious, and...pure evil."

"Grandmother," Bree answered, "I appreciate the fact that you're concerned about me, and I do take your warning seriously. I've been extra careful; I even bought a deadbolt lock for my apartment door. I'll be okay. I don't want you to worry about me."

Grandmother smiled. "Worrying is what I do best. Just ask Denver. He will tell you."

When Denver walked Bree to her car, he seemed anxious. "What did the two of you talk about?"

"She just wanted to warn me herself to be careful. Your grandmother is such a sweet lady."

Denver nodded and looked relieved.

"But," Bree continued, "between the two of you, I'm going to be jumping at my own shadow pretty soon. Last night I heard something rustling in the bushes and I about leapt a mile. It was probably a rabbit or something."

"I'm sorry. The last thing I want is for you to be scared all the time."

Bree was about to respond, but Denver guided her gently against the car. His mouth was on hers in a devouring kiss as he wrapped his arms around her, leaning his body against hers. She felt the heat of desire burning within her as his hands explored the contours of her body. Everything else in the world ceased to exist for the moment except the two of them and their passion.

"I want you, Bree," he said, whispering in her ear.

Bree's heart was pounding. "I want you too," she answered, losing herself in his embrace.

"Let's go back to your apartment."

Bree thought about it. She imagined their bodies together, skin touching skin, and how wonderful it would be.

"It sounds good to me, but it's pretty late. What reason would you give Grandmother for leaving?"

"We'd tell her we want to make wild, passionate love together, all night long."

Bree laughed, feeling the heat rush to her face. "We can't tell her that!"

"She was young once. I'm sure she'd understand," he answered, laughing. "Seriously, I'll just say I'll be back in a while. She won't ask questions."

The idea of their two bodies melting into one excited Bree. "If you're sure it's okay."

"Ohh, I'm sure."

"Well then, I'll head on home and see you in a few."

"Sounds great," he said, giving her a kiss and running towards the house.

CHAPTER FIVE

Bree's life seemed to be going smoothly. Even though no commitments had been made, her relationship with Denver was heading in the right direction. Being with him made her happy. Even going to work was more enjoyable.

She was standing at the bar giving Larry her drink orders when Sheila came over.

"Well, lucky you," Sheila said. "The hunk is back, and he's at one of your tables."

"Which one?"

"Table four."

Bree turned around casually. The man was in his mid-twenties, with blue eyes and short, layered blond hair, bangs stylishly falling along the side of his face. His tattoos drew attention to his thick biceps, especially the one of a naked mermaid sitting on and clinging to an anchor. He had rugged good looks and his smug attitude suggested he knew it.

"He's been here before? He doesn't look familiar to me."

"He was here the night of the storm when you almost hit that woman. He couldn't take his eyes off you. He's kind of cute, too."

"I guess so," she said, with an air of indifference.

Sheila laughed. "You sure are smitten with that Denver dude, aren't you? A Brad Pitt look-alike comes in and you don't even bat an eye."

Bree smiled as she went over to the table to wait on the stranger. "Hi, my name's Bree. I'll be your waitress," she said, handing him a menu. "Can I get you something to drink?"

He leisurely leaned back in his chair, tilted his head, and looked Bree up and down. His lower lip protruded slightly as he grinned with his eyes.

"When you're ready to order, let me know," Bree said, glaring at him before turning to leave.

"I know where your father is."

Bree stopped and looked back at him. His cocky grin was irritating. "I know where my father is, too. What's your point?"

"Now, come on—Brianna," he said, slowly emphasizing her name. "We both know I'm not talking about your adoptive father."

Bree's heart raced. No one up here, except Denver, knew of her adoption. "What makes you think I was adopted?"

"I was hired by your real father to find you. He's been searching for you for years."

Speechless, Bree tried processing what she'd just heard. "Look, if this is your idea of a joke—"

"Trust me. It's no joke."

"Why should I believe you? What proof do you have?"

"I have a picture of your father, if you'd like to see it." He held out the picture to her.

She took the photo reluctantly and stared at it. She saw a man of average build with straight dark hair—graying slightly, intense eyes, and a square-shaped jaw. She kept looking at him, as if he might tell her something. Flinging the picture down, she put her hands on the table and leaned forward. "This proves nothing. He doesn't even look like me." She turned to storm away, but he grabbed her wrist.

"I have another picture you may be interested in."

"Is there a problem here?" Larry asked in a gruff voice.

"There's no problem," the man said, letting go of her wrist. "I was just showing Brianna some pictures."

"It's okay, Larry. I appreciate your help, but after I get a few things straight with him, he'll be leaving."

Larry hesitated, then went back to the bar.

Bree sat down. "First, who the hell are you?"

"Scott."

"Show me ID."

He handed her his New York driver's license. *Scott Proctor* was the name given. "You've got spunk, Miss Brianna. I like that."

"Does my father know what kind of sleaze he's hired? You're not exactly the kind of person most dads would send after their daughter."

"I can be professional when I have to. Just thought you and I could mix a little pleasure with business."

"Let me see the other picture, then you're out of here."

Scott slowly withdrew it, as if unveiling some precious jewel.

Bree snatched it. There was a man, obviously the same man in the previous picture, but around twenty years younger with a healthier color to his skin. He was holding a little girl with deep brown curly hair. Next to him was a woman with the same dark curly hair, only longer. They were all smiling; the little girl looked like the early pictures Bree had of herself.

Bree tried blinking back the tears. Feelings of abandonment came flooding to the surface, feelings she didn't even know existed within her.

"Why?" she said softly. "Why did they leave me?" Her vulnerability was open, exposed.

"How should I know? He wants me to set up a time and place to meet. Do you want to see him or not?"

Bree's mind reeled. So many thoughts were overtaking her, it was hard to concentrate. She wanted to meet him, but where? A crowded place wouldn't be good in case things got emotional, yet she didn't want it to be secluded either. Wanting to meet her father, but not quite trusting Scott, she decided on the marina. It was a safe place because Denver had a lot of friends there who would look out for her. Yet, they could take a walk down the dock for privacy.

"What about tomorrow evening, seven o'clock at the marina?"

"That's fine. He'll be there."

"What's his name?"

"Louis. Louis Cipriano."

Bree stared as he walked away. Was it possible she would be meeting her real father? Tears started to flow.

Bree walked over to Larry. "Since business is slow, can I have the afternoon off?"

"Sure. Are you okay? What did that man want?"

Through a half-laugh and half-cry, she managed to respond, "I'm going to meet someone."

Anxious to tell someone, Bree drove straight to Denver's house and pounded on his door.

Denver came quickly and opened it. When he saw Bree standing there all excited, like a child on Christmas morning, he had to laugh. "What's got you so riled up?"

"Something happened today. This man, Scott, came into the bar and told me that he works for my father, my birth father, who has been looking for me for years. He wants to meet me tomorrow night. Isn't that great?"

Denver frowned. "I don't know, Bree. I don't like it."

"What's not to like? I thought you'd be happy for me."

"Someone shows up, claiming to know your father, and you're ready to go off and meet him just like that. Did you get this guy's ID?"

"Of course," she said, crossing her arms. "He's from New York, and his name's Scott Proctor."

"How do you know the man you're meeting tomorrow is your father?"

"He had these pictures," she said, handing them to him.

"Wow!" he said, staring at the photos. "No wonder you're excited. She looks like you."

"See? What did I tell you?"

"I don't know. I still have doubts. Don't go tomorrow. We need to have him checked out first."

"I don't believe you. I thought you'd be the one who would understand my need to know where I came from. I already told him I'd be there. I'm going."

"Bree," he said, grabbing her shoulders. "Listen to me. You may not take Grandmother's warnings seriously, but anyone who knows her well does. She's rarely wrong. Please, don't go."

"I have to. Besides, the danger Grandmother saw could be anything. She wasn't clear on any details."

Denver looked at her, his face contorted. "Okay. Would you at least let me go with you?"

"Fine, pick me up at six thirty. We're meeting at the marina at seven o'clock."

"Okay," he agreed, feeling good about the location at least.

CHAPTER SIX

The next day, Bree was restless and wished the meeting was earlier. The hour hand took an eternity to move. Too much time to think. What should she wear to meet her father? Rummaging through her closet and dresser, she tossed different combinations on the bed, then put them back, narrowing her choices. No to dresses or anything too fancy—they were meeting at the marina. No to shorts or jeans—too casual. Finally, she chose beige dress slacks and a burgundy blouse. Now for jewelry. Something subtle, yet elegant. Perfect. Shoes? Definitely not heels—walking on the dock would be treacherous. Flats it was. Hair? Would love to leave it down, but with the lake breeze, putting it up in a hair clip would be best...

Bree bit her nails. "Stop it," she said to herself.

What would they talk about? "Hey, what about them Tigers, Dad?" she joked to herself. He probably wouldn't know about Detroit baseball. She had truckloads of unanswered questions, but would it be appropriate to ask them this soon?

She was ready early and thinking too much. Her stomach felt like an alien had taken up residence inside her.

Bree watched out the window and saw Denver arrive. She met him at the door before he had time to knock. "Let's go," she said, hurrying past him.

"What kind of greeting is that?" he said, laughing.

"Oh, I'm sorry," Bree said, smiling as she kissed him. "I guess I'm excited. And a little nervous."

"I'm nervous myself, but for other reasons."

"I don't see what you're worried about. Why would my father want to hurt me? And if he isn't my father, what would he gain by saying that he is? It's not like I'm a rich heiress or something."

"I don't have the answers. Maybe it's all legit and everything will work out great, but I want you to be careful."

Bree shook her head. "You sure are protective, aren't you?"

Denver frowned, started the jeep, and drove to the marina in silence. On the dock, they could feel the cool breeze coming off the lake. Denver stood behind Bree, wrapping his arms around her.

"I'm glad you came," Bree said. "It would've been torture to wait alone."

He gave her a little squeeze and kissed the top of her head.

"Brianna?" came a heavily accented voice from behind them. Turning around, she recognized the man from the picture.

"Yes, I'm Brianna. Are you Louis?"

"Yes, I am Louis, your papa," he said, hesitating for a moment before reaching out to hug her. "Brianna," he continued, choking back tears. "It has been so long. I thought I would never find you."

Bree wrapped her arms around him, tears streaming down her cheeks as she eagerly nodded that she understood.

"Look at you," he said. "My little Brianna is a woman now. You look just like your mama did at your age."

Bree nervously laughed and dabbed at her eyes. "I don't know what to say. You're really my father?"

Louis grinned, happily. "I most definitely am. Finally, my search for you has ended. It has been unbearable not knowing even if you were alive."

"That must have been awful for you."

"Yes, yes, but the search is now over and that is what matters."

Bree listened as he talked. The accent sounded familiar. "Italian?" she asked. "Are you Italian?"

"Yes, I am."

"What about my mother? Is she Italian, too?"

"Yes. We are from Italy, where you were born."

Bree began to laugh. "Do you hear that, Denver? You're dating an Italian. I'm Italian," she repeated, absorbing this new piece of information.

"Oh," she said, finally remembering her manners. "I forgot to introduce you. Louis," she said slowly, not comfortable yet with calling him Dad. But, calling him 'Louis' didn't feel right either. "This is my friend Denver. Denver, this is Louis."

Denver extended his hand. "Nice to meet you."

Louis clasped his hand and gave it a firm shake. "My name is Louis Cipriano. I trust you have been treating my Brianna well."

"I've been trying my best. I hope you don't mind my asking, but this has happened suddenly. Do you have a birth certificate or some other proof of your relationship?"

"Denver," Bree said, "what are you doing?"

Louis laughed. "That is alright, Brianna. He cares for you. I am glad you have such a good friend. To answer your question—no, I do not have anything with me. I will call home immediately and have a copy of Brianna's birth certificate sent. I should have thought of it myself, but when I received news that my little girl had been found, I had to come right away. I did not think of such things."

"Well," Denver said, excusing himself. "I'm going to wait over on the Nighthawk so you two can talk. You have a lot of catching up to do, and I'm sure Bree has a hundred questions to ask. I wish you luck."

Bree gave him a playful slug as he departed. But he was right. Actually, there were zillions of questions buzzing around in her head.

They sat on a bench and talked for over an hour, trying to recapture the lost years. Bringing the conversation around to family, Louis spoke of her grandparents, aunts, and uncles.

"They are eager to see you again. Someday you must come to Italy to meet your family, but for now I am going to be selfish. I want this time for myself, to get to know you again."

Bree agreed. Going to Italy would be exciting, but meeting her father was enough to deal with right now.

Changing the subject, she presented the questions that weighed heaviest on her mind. "Why was I abandoned, and where is my mother now?"

"Ah," he said, nodding. "I knew you would want to know these things, but they are hard to explain. Where should I begin?" he mused, taking a moment before continuing. "We Italians have a certain passion for life. I hope you do not think less of me, but I was not the husband I should have been. I had an affair. Your mama found out and went into a rage. To hurt me, she took you and fled. I felt terrible about the pain she suffered and never stopped looking for both of you, but to search in America never entered my mind. Patrizia, your mama, came from a poor family. How she managed to come here and hide you, I can only guess. I looked all over Europe—having reason to believe that's where you were—but let's not bother with all that now."

Bree was silent, taking everything in. Why would a mother abandon her child because of an affair? She must have loved him deeply, almost to the point of obsession. It didn't make any sense, but then she had heard of people doing all kinds of desperate things in the name of love.

"As for her location," he continued. "There is someone working on that. It should not be long before we find her. My thoughts used to be that when I found her, I would have her arrested. She deserves jail time for what we have been through, but it all seems foolish now. I have my daughter, and how would I look if I put your mama in jail? I do, however, insist on an explanation," he said, staring off into the distance. "I promise you. We will have that."

After sharing more stories, Louis reluctantly got up, handing Bree a slip of paper. "This is my number. I will be here a few more days. If you need anything, call me. We can meet tomorrow, perhaps?"

"Yes, I would like that," Bree said. They made arrangements and said goodbye.

Awkwardly, they both hesitated before turning to leave.

Overwhelmed, Louis extended his arms. "My darling daughter, I hope you don't mind, but I must have one more hug. I have waited so long for this day."

With happy tears streaming down her face, Bree stepped forward into his comforting embrace. He held on like he didn't want to let go.

After a moment, they reluctantly released each other and again said goodbye.

Bree walked over to the Nighthawk. Denver stopped what he was doing and jumped over the rail, onto the dock. "So, how'd everything go?"

"Wonderful. I've learned a lot about myself."

"That's good. I know how important this was to you. Your father seemed sincere."

"See? I told you not to worry."

When she started relaying the whole conversation, Denver frowned. "It doesn't make sense. I don't buy it. A mother doesn't abandon her child like that."

"Haven't you read the papers lately? A baby was just found in a dumpster—left by its mother!"

"Yes, that's true, but the woman in the picture didn't look capable of that. She had kind eyes, like yours."

Even though Bree knew she only had Louis's version of things, she was not about to admit it to Denver. She was beginning to get irritated with his negativity.

"Just promise me that until we see the birth certificate, you won't go off alone with Louis and you'll stay away from Scott Proctor. If you want to meet Louis somewhere, make sure it's in a public place or here at the marina. I would feel a lot better if you could promise me that."

"Okay," she said. "I feel like I have three fathers now," she added as she turned away.

Denver understood he had pushed her as far as he could. He couldn't tell Bree, but he was going to check Louis's story out.

A MOTHER'S SACRIFICE

CHAPTER SEVEN

Halfway around the world, in Marseille, France, Patrizia sat silently at her kitchen table, biting her nails. She didn't realize it, but she had bitten them right down to the skin. The last fifteen years had been agonizing. She had tried to get on with her life, but thoughts of the daughter she had given up would come to her mind, overwhelming her at unexpected times. She learned to accept that Brianna's birthday and holidays would be spent in unrelenting tears, but it was those other moments when a memory would come to visit at uninvited times that would emotionally demolish her. Even though Louis was in prison, she never even had peace for her safety. Often, she felt like she was being watched. With his connections, it was possible. The little peace that she did have was about to end. Her good friend Elise always kept her informed of what was going on. Louis would be released from prison soon.

Patrizia tried to think clearly and make plans, but she was too petrified. She was sure he would come looking for her as soon as he was free. She remembered when the police had slapped the handcuffs on him and hauled him away, all those years ago. He had spit at her and sworn vengeance. The anger and hatred in his voice had caused her to shake so violently, she'd required sedation to calm down.

There wasn't anyone special in Patrizia's life. Her previous bad experiences with two men had made her leery to try her luck a third time. Besides, she had learned the hard way that anyone she got involved with was being put in danger. Louis never cared who got in the way. That young Italian man who had tried to help her... he'd paid for it with his life.

Patrizia thought back to when it all started and her life took a turn for the worse....

The first mistake she'd made was during her first year at the University of Naples. She had studied hard to keep her grades up so she could continue her schooling. She came from a poor farming family, but as long as her grades and testing scores met the school's standards, she would be granted admission.

She had been so full of hope about what her future might hold. She liked her freedom and enjoyed studying for a career. Perhaps she enjoyed it a little too much. She met her good friend Elise there. Elise was a spirited young woman from France, with light-brown hair and an upturned nose, full of devilry. Elise studied abroad in Italy, mainly to get away from home and have some fun. Her family was wealthy and paid her expenses.

They got caught up in the campus social life, and Patrizia became enamored with a young man she was seeing. Things were going great until she learned she was pregnant. He then wanted nothing more to do with Patrizia or the child. She was devastated. How could she raise a child alone and continue her education?

During this low point in her life, she met Louis. He was six years older than her, and sophisticated; being wrapped up in her worries, Patrizia barely noticed his advances towards her, but Louis was infatuated with her and did not give up so easily. He loved her long, flowing hair and the graceful way she walked. He would visit her every day, bringing candy or flowers.

Patrizia was flattered that such an attractive, worldly man would be interested in her. He was a successful businessman from a wealthy family, and pursued Patrizia with fervor. She found his persistence charming, feeling cherished and protected. She even told him she was expecting a child, but it didn't matter to him. He loved her and wanted to take care of her and her baby.

She could not believe her good fortune, finding someone like Louis at a time when she needed someone the most. She had to be the luckiest person on Earth. He wined and dined her, and when he proposed he even had tears in his eyes.

They were married after only knowing each other a few months. It was a small wedding ceremony, with only a few close friends and immediate family.

Patrizia and Louis were happy together at first. They lived in an apartment in the city. When the baby was born, they named her Brianna and listed Louis on the birth certificate as the father. But it didn't take long before Louis started to change.

He would yell and curse at the littlest things. At first Patrizia would yell right back. But one day, he slapped her and told her he would not have a tramp like her being disrespectful to him.

As time went by his moods became uglier, more erratic. Eventually Patrizia threatened to leave him. He was sitting on a chair holding Brianna when she did.

"Ah," he said to the baby he was bouncing on his lap. "Your mama thinks she is going to leave me. What do you think of that, little one? Does she not know there is nowhere she could go that I would not find her? Then of course I would have to make her pay," he added smugly, "and you, too."

The baby, of course, didn't understand what was being said. She laughed gleefully.

"Yes," he said, smiling at her. "It is an amusing thought."

"You would not hurt Brianna, would you?" Patrizia asked, horrified.

Louis's tone changed, and he said brusquely, "That decision is up to you."

Patrizia sank down in a chair. He was holding the ace that would keep her trapped forever. They both knew she could never leave. Louis laughed when he looked over at Patrizia and saw her slumped down helplessly in the chair. Chills shook her body.

As time passed, Louis stopped trying to conceal from Patrizia the nature of his business. In front of her he would be on the phone discussing drug transactions and shipments of merchandise. He even discussed in detail methods of persuasion, laughing as she would abruptly get up and leave the room.

Patrizia endured her marriage the best she could. She tried to please Louis by keeping the apartment spotless and having meals ready for him when he got home. But it never really mattered. If he was in one of his moods, he could always find something wrong to use as an excuse to take out his aggression on her. She lived each day knowing that her world could be shattered in an instant.

Brianna was almost two years old when things became intolerable. Louis came home one night angry at the world. He complained about dinner. "What do you call this?" he asked, knocking his plate on the floor. "It is like eating a dish rag. There is no flavor!" Patrizia quickly bent down to clean up the mess.

"I work hard all day and I come home to this," he said, waving his arm angrily in the air. He looked at little Brianna, who had been startled by the crashing plate and was sucking her thumb. "I guess, Brianna, this is what I get for marrying a slut. Did you know that your mother is a slut?"

She stared up at him with big eyes.

"Please, Louis," Patrizia pleaded as she stood up. "Do not talk about me like that to her."

"Oh," he chided. "You do not think your daughter needs to know the truth? Pregnant and not even married. What does that make you?"

"Stop," she said, "I can stand no more."

"You? You?" he asked. "You are lucky to have me. Who would have wanted you the way you were? You should be down on your knees thanking me. Go on, get down on your knees."

"I will not, Louis," she said, letting her pride get in her way. "Please, leave me alone."

"I told you to get down on your knees!" he yelled, grabbing a handful of her hair. She screamed as he yanked her to the floor. "Now thank me."

Patrizia was sobbing now. "Thank you," she said meekly.

He picked her up and slammed her against the wall. "Thank you, Louis, for marrying a slut like me. Say it!"

"Thank you, Louis," she started, but she was sobbing too hard to get any more words out. When she saw his fist coming towards her, she took a deep breath and turned her head, bracing herself for the pain. She slumped down to the floor. As darkness came over her like a veil, she could faintly feel him kicking her. Then she felt nothing. Patrizia woke up in the hospital. She had some bruised ribs and a mild concussion. It hurt to move. It even hurt to breathe.

"How did this happen?" the doctor asked.

Patrizia opened her mouth to speak, but she felt a stabbing pain. Lines creased her forehead. She was trying to hold back tears. It hurt too much to cry. "Ask Louis," she finally managed to get out.

The doctor looked frustrated. He had seen cases like this before and knew she would not talk. "He brought you here. According to him, you were riding a bicycle downhill, lost control, and hit a tree. Is that how it happened?"

She turned her head and stared out the window. It hurt to talk, and she just wanted everything to go away.

The doctor closed his chart. "We will get you something for the pain," he said, patting her on the leg. "Try to get some sleep."

After the painkillers kicked in, she drifted off to sleep. When she woke up, Louis was at her side. She winced when she saw him. It was an involuntary reaction; he would never touch her with people coming and going from her room. He was much too clever for that.

"I am sorry, Patrizia. Sometimes I get so upset I lose control. I did not mean to hurt you. I promise it will not happen again." He sounded so sincere that she might have believed him. But they had been through this before. He would be charming and sweet for a while, but things would inevitably go back to the way they were.

She did not answer. There was no energy for life left in her. She could feel herself slipping into a sea of despair. "You should have just finished me off, Louis," she said in a hollow, emotionless voice. "It would have been the nicest thing you ever did for me."

Louis could see he was not getting anywhere, so he left. There would be plenty of time later to make her see things his way.

Elise had been out in the waiting room. After Louis left, she went in to see Patrizia. She stood there shaking her head. "What did he do to you?" Elise asked, trying to fight back tears as she paced back and forth at her friend's bedside. "There will be no end to this, Patrizia. You must leave him—you must!"

Patrizia stared blankly at her friend. How could she explain that she was even more scared to leave than to stay? She could handle dying, but she could not handle the thought of Brianna being hurt.

Elise walked over to the door and looked down the hallway to make sure no one was listening.

"It is Brianna, is it not?" she questioned. "If you only had yourself to think of, you could take the chance and leave. You would be no worse off than you are already, but you are afraid for Brianna. Am I right?"

Patrizia did not have to answer. The fear in her eyes told Elise all she needed to know.

"I have been thinking about your problem for a long time. In my mind, I went over every detail again and again. There is only one solution. We must hide you and Brianna away from that swine."

"No. He would not give up until he found us. With his connections, there is nowhere to hide."

"Let him search forever if he wishes," said Elise. "He will never find you. I have a plan. Just hear what I must say and think on it for a time. The only thing I do not like is that you will have to go back home for a few days. I hate the idea, but I see no other way for you to get Brianna. After you are home for a little while, Louis will relax and think things are normal again. He is an arrogant man, and will not suspect a thing," she said through gritted teeth, glancing towards the door. "You will say you are going to get your hair done, and you will bring Brianna with you. I have the key to a friend's apartment. We will go there, and swap identities: I will be you. I am having a long brunette wig made up to look just like your hair. I will cut your hair and color it to make yours lighter, just like the passport my papa has for you. With these changes and the lightly tinted glasses I have for you, you should not have any trouble getting through customs."

"How can I leave? Mama and Papa will be sick with worry if we just disappear. I cannot put them through that."

"I know. It would be hard. They love you very much and would not stop looking for you."

"Maybe I could fill out some postcards that you can drop in the mail from different locations. They will know we are alive."

"Yes, yes, that is a great idea."

"Elise," Patrizia interrupted, overwhelmed with fear. "I do not know why I am talking like this. It would never work. I do not have the energy to fight him. He is too powerful. I am nothing."

"You cannot keep living like this," Elise said, getting angry. "He will not stop until he kills you, and he would find a way to make it look like an accident. Then who will protect Brianna? Would you prefer that Louis bring her up alone?"

Patrizia panicked. She had not thought about that at all. Brianna being raised alone by Louis was frightening. Her heart began to race. "No, that must never happen. I will not let that happen."

"Then let me tell you more about my plan. We cannot be seen together. I will arrive at the apartment ahead of you and will have the clothes and everything else we will need laid out. You should not bring anything, not even a toothbrush. Only bring Brianna. You cannot do anything to give yourself away. Absolutely no packing. We will leave the apartment at different times. I will have tickets and passports ready for you both to fly to the United States under assumed names: Brianna's passport gives her name as Anna. While you are getting away, I plan on leading Louis all over Europe using your name."

"I can give you some of my checks," Patrizia said. "If you start using them around my mama's hometown, he will think I left Brianna with my relatives. Lucky for us, I come from a big family. That should keep him busy for a time."

"Yes, that is a great idea."

Elise stopped for a moment. Patrizia was holding her side and taking deep breaths. She knew this was not a suitable time to be springing this on her, but it was the only way. Patrizia was like a sister to her, the best friend she'd ever had. For the last two years Elise had watched the lively spirit in her friend slowly die. She knew they had to do it now, or it might end up being too late.

Patrizia laid still for a while, and her breathing slowly returned to normal. "Elise, I do not want you involved. You would be putting yourself in danger."

"Me?" Elise asked, looking surprised. "He will not have a clue who I am. When I think I have given you enough time, I will go back to being myself. You will disappear like vapor. I know you so well, I can act and look like you better than you can. We are almost the same in size, no? I will walk, talk, and dress like you. You know how I love a little mischief. I will take immense pleasure in making him the fool."

Patrizia gave her friend a faint smile. She remembered all the fun they used to have, all the pranks they had pulled on people. Elise was always up to something, and Patrizia knew that even though it would be dangerous, Elise would love the thrill of it.

"You need your rest," Elise said, looking concerned. "I will leave so you can sleep. You do not have to make a decision now and the choice, of course, is yours. I just want you to know that you do have an option if it gets to where you have to make that decision. I want to have everything ready and in place. Do not even think about it right now. Just get some sleep."

Patrizia nodded. She was lucky to have such a good friend.

Elise walked out into the hallway and hunted down the doctor. She confirmed what he already had suspected. "Could you arrange to keep Patrizia in the hospital as long as possible? Even a few extra days will help. I fear for her safety. She needs more time to heal."

"I will do what I can, but I cannot keep her here forever. I will order extra tests. That will give you a couple more days."

"Thank you," Elise said to him, shaking his hand in gratitude. "You do not know what a help that will be."

Elise went home and could not sleep at all that night. She feared she had not convinced Patrizia of anything. Staying could only mean misery for Patrizia and Briannna, but how could she convince Patrizia of that?

The next night when Elise went to see Patrizia, she looked a little better. Though still aching all over, she was in a better mood and took interest in Elise's plan. She knew it would never work, but even the slightest hope of a way out cheered her up.

While Elise kept Louis believing he was chasing Patrizia in Europe, Patrizia and Brianna would make their escape to the States.

"What will I do when I get there and how will I support both of us?" she asked.

"Papa has your papers ready and assures me they will not be questioned. You will be able to look for a home and a job."

"I do not know if I can do this," Patrizia said. "Louis will be furious. If he catches us..."

"You must listen to me," Elise pleaded. "This is not the end of the beatings. He will not change—this you know. If something happens to you, Brianna will be left in Louis's care. What kind of life do you think she will have? If you do somehow survive, is that what you want Brianna to see and grow up with? They say if you grow up with abuse, there is a good chance you will marry someone abusive."

Patrizia knew everything Elise said was true.

"You do not need to decide now. After you have been home a few days, call me if you change your mind. But you must remember, once you decide to do this, there will be no turning back. We will have no choice but to go through with it."

Patrizia was silent. Leaving and possibly bringing Louis's wrath on them terrified her, but if she stayed, he might someday go too far.

CHAPTER EIGHT

A few days later, Patrizia was released from the hospital. They put her left arm in a sling to reduce movement. With the help of pain medicine, her head felt better and the bruised ribs were tolerable as long as she didn't move suddenly.

When they arrived home, Louis paid the babysitter while Patrizia went into the living room to look for Brianna. She found her sitting alone in the middle of the floor, playing with her toys.

"Hi, baby," Patrizia said.

Brianna stopped playing and looked up. At first, she stared at her mother like she was a stranger.

"Brianna, it's your mama," Patrizia said to her, holding her arm out.

Brianna's eyes grew big and she ran to Patrizia. She clung to her mama's leg so tightly, Patrizia winced from the pain. "I have missed you so much, honey."

Patrizia helped Brianna climb up on her lap. She hugged her, then she noticed bruises on her arm. Turning, she looked up at Louis.

"She is spoiled," Louis said. "She would not stop crying." He left the room as if that explained everything.

Later, when Louis was upstairs, Patrizia showed Brianna some of her bruises. "See," she said, "Mama has bruises." Then she pointed to Brianna's bruises. "You have some too. Can you tell me how you got those bruises?"

Brianna hung her head. "Papa."

"Papa gave you those bruises?"

Brianna nodded. "I'm a bad girl," she said and stuck her thumb in her mouth.

"No, no. You are not a bad girl. Look at me," Patrizia said, gently lifting her head up. "You are a good girl. Papa was bad." Then she rocked Brianna on her lap, while wiping at her tears.

Patrizia spent the afternoon with Brianna, not letting her out of her sight.

When it was time for bed, Patrizia went to put Brianna in her crib. She had to peel her from her and set her down. Brianna gave a terrible shriek. "Mama. Stay, stay!" Patrizia went back to pick her up.

"Leave her there," said Louis from the doorway behind her.

"But she is scared."

"She will cry herself to sleep soon enough. She always does."

"Brianna, honey," Patrizia said, trying to comfort her. "I am going to be down the hall in my bedroom. I will see you in the morning. Now go to sleep."

"No, Mama. Stay!" she cried louder. It brought tears to Patrizia's eyes as she left and went down the hallway.

Louis and Patrizia laid in bed, listening to the wailing coming from down the hall. Brianna sounded terrified.

Patrizia tried to block it out. "I have to get her, Louis," she finally said, starting to get out of bed.

"I said leave her!"

Patrizia was familiar enough with that tone of his voice to know it was useless. She laid back down in bed with her fists clenched in anger. How could he be so cold and unsympathetic? She was not even allowed to comfort her child when she was scared. What kind of monster was he? She could only imagine how Brianna got those bruises and how terrified she must have been. The more she listened in the dark to Brianna's pleas, the more the feelings of hate for Louis began to grow inside of her. Hate for the man lying next to her filled her veins like poisonous venom. She now had a clear picture of what Brianna's future would be like. She had to do it. Every cry she heard hardened her resolve. She had to give Brianna a chance at having a normal, happy life.

The next day Patrizia called Elise, careful of what she said. "I have been thinking about what you suggested. Having my hair done is exactly what I need. I will make my appointment for Thursday. That will give me a couple more days to get rested so I will have some energy back for a day out."

"Oui," said Elise, knowing that Louis must still be home. "I am glad that you are taking my advice."

Patrizia found a reason to quickly end the conversation. She broke out in a nervous sweat, and her stomach felt nauseous. She could not believe she was going to do it.

When Thursday came, Patrizia got herself and Brianna ready to leave after Louis went to work. She remembered what Elise had said and brought nothing with them except her purse and Brianna's favorite blanket. Louis had lots of friends in the neighborhood that would get curious if she walked out with a suitcase. Louis was good at putting on a front for people. Everyone thought he was such a charming, sweet man. She could not blame them for being taken in by his act. She had fallen for it herself when she first met him. It was almost as if he were two people.

She drove to the address Elise had given her in the hospital. Brianna sat next to her, chattering away. She seemed excited about going on a trip with her mama. When they got to the apartment and went inside, Patrizia and Elise gently hugged.

"Are you sure you want to do this?" Patrizia asked. "By helping me, you are putting yourself in real danger. I do not feel good about that."

"Nonsense. You know that no one can pack, move, or travel faster than I. Whenever I use your name at a hotel or anywhere, I will quickly be out of there and not even stay for the night. It will just be a diversion to throw Louis off. I will enjoy giving that snake a hard time. He deserves it," she said, smiling at the thought of Louis being on the receiving end for a change.

"I am afraid for you. How will I know if you are okay? Is there a number I can call you at?"

Elise thought a moment, then scribbled a number on a piece of paper. "Here. Memorize this number and destroy the paper. In two weeks, on Friday, my time, call me at 7:00 pm. I will be there to receive your call."

"Okay," Patrizia said, putting the slip of paper in her pocket. "Thank you for everything you are doing."

Elise waved her hand like it was no big deal. "There is one more matter to discuss though. You cannot call me Elise anymore. I am Patrizia, no? We need to start using our new names now to get accustomed to it."

"Of course—Patrizia—I remember. This is going to be strange."

Elise gave Patrizia the passport she'd had made for her. "I am cutting your hair to match this style. With your new slightly tinted glasses, matching hair style and color, you will resemble her enough no one will question it." She got out the scissors and started cutting Patrizia's hair. "I do not like cutting your hair off. It is so gorgeous."

Elise then started giggling. "I feel like we are back in school. Remember how we used to work on each other's hair, trying the latest styles?"

"Yes, I do. Those were good times."

Brianna watched the two with interest. She didn't understand what was going on, but she could sense the excitement in the air. Whenever they would laugh, she would laugh, too.

When Elise finished cutting Patrizia's hair, she dyed it, dried, and styled it. "You look great with short hair. You should have tried it sooner."

"Louis would not have it," Patrizia said bitterly. "He likes my hair long, and he does not like bangs either. I had no choice."

"Those days are over, Elise. Now, here are the clothes you will wear and your new glasses. You can change in the bedroom and I will change in the bathroom. Then we will see how we did."

When they came out they both looked at each other and burst into laughter. Patrizia's short hairstyle emphasized her high cheekbones and the fullness of her lips, making her facial features more pronounced. The clothes she had on were brightly colored and form-fitting. They were nothing at all like anything Patrizia ever wore. The tinted glasses she had on really set the whole thing off.

Elise wore a long skirt and a long-sleeved white blouse. She had her contacts in and had put on the wig.

"Oh, I need one more thing," Elise commented. She picked up the sling that was lying on the table and put it on. She limped around the kitchen moaning and put one hand to her forehead.

Patrizia laughed. "Am I that pathetic?"

"Only that first day in the hospital. Sorry, I could not resist. I need to practice if I am going to convince people I am you. It does not hurt for me to keep in mind that I am still recovering from injuries. I hope the trip is not too hard on you."

"I will be fine. I will just have to take it easy." She turned to look at her daughter. "So, Brianna. What do you think of your mama now?"

She walked over to Brianna, who whined and ran away from her. "Brianna," she tried again. "It is me, your mama."

Brianna looked up at the two of them, confused.

"I will go in the bathroom and take the wig off until the two of you are gone," Elise said.

It took a little convincing, but finally Brianna accepted Patrizia as her mother.

When Elise came out of the bathroom, she went over the last details with Patrizia. She told her what airport to go to and gave her Brianna's passport. "Remember, you must call Brianna 'Anna.' They are very observant."

"Where do I go after I get to America?" Patrizia asked.

"That decision will be up to you. The less I know about where you go after that point, the safer the two of you will be. I suggest you put some distance between you and New York, just in case Louis does look for you there."

"That is good advice," Patrizia said, and sighed. For a few hours she had forgotten how dangerous what she was doing was, but now the fearful feelings started to creep back in. "Am I doing the right thing? Can we pull this off?"

"Listen to me. This is the best thing for both of you. You could not divorce him. He told you what he would do if you did, and legally he is Brianna's father. You would have to let him see her. You do not have a choice."

Patrizia started to cry. "I hope you know how much I appreciate all your help. You have always been there for me."

Elise started crying, too, and they gave each other a hug. "My father offered to pay your expenses and handle the details. I did not tell him about me being a decoy. He might not have agreed to that part of our plan."

Patrizia wiped the tears from her eyes and told Elise goodbye. She grabbed the handle and began to pull the suitcase that Elise had ready for her. "I can only imagine what wild things you have inside here for me to wear."

They gave each other another hug and said their final goodbyes. Switching vehicles, Patrizia left first, Elise left a while after.

It was a long trip through Italy. Patrizia traveled on the viaduct that wound its way through the mountains. She had always taken the beauty of her native country for granted, but knowing she may never see it again made her look at it differently. Patrizia took in the mountain slopes and summits that cut against the sky. The landscape was covered with lush green forests, and the snow-capped mountain peaks reached up into the clouds. Traveling was what Patrizia had always wanted to do, but she'd always thought that Italy would be her home. Her heart ached to think of leaving her beloved country and family behind, but she had to do what was best for Brianna.

Crossing the border of Italy into France was not a problem. At the airport, however, Patrizia was worried. As the man was checking their passports, Brianna patted Patrizia on the face. "Look Mama, plane." She had spoken in Italian, but the passports said they were French. The man looked at them, then back at the names on the passports.

Patrizia smiled and tried to act casual. "Yes, Anna," she said carefully in her best French. "That is a plane."

He shrugged, giving them back their passports and letting them pass. Patrizia let out a sigh of relief when she sat down in the plane. She was glad she had taken courses in English whenever possible. From Elise she had also learned French. The little education she'd had was definitely coming in handy now.

When they reached the United States, she took a taxi to her hotel room. It was late when they arrived and Patrizia was exhausted. Feeling a little jet-lagged, she went right to bed and slept most of the next day, with Brianna snuggled up next to her. Patrizia smiled at her. "I love you, Brianna," she said, and sang to her the lullaby that had become a tradition with them.

Fa la ninna, fa la nanna
Nella braccia della mamma
Fa la ninna bel bambina,
Fa la nanna bambina bel,
Fa la ninna, fa la nanna
Nella braccia della mamma.

Brianna was sucking her thumb, but she smiled at her and patted her face as if to say, "I love you too, Mama."

CHAPTER NINE

The following morning, Patrizia slept in so late she had to rush to be checked out by the eleven o'clock deadline. Between traveling and crossing several time zones, she was exhausted. They took a taxi to the train station and boarded a train to Ohio. She felt better putting some distance between them and New York.

Patrizia and Brianna stayed at another motel. She decided not to start job and apartment searching until she could call Elise and know she was alright. Her nerves were too shot to think of much else.

When the time came, Patrizia nervously made the call. When Elise answered, she was frantic—not her usual calm at all.

"Patrizia, are you alright?"

"Yes."

"And Brianna?"

"Yes, Brianna and I are fine. What is the matter?"

"Are you sure you were not followed?"

"Yes, yes, we are fine and we are not being followed. What is going on? You are scaring me."

"What a relief! I have been out of my head with fright! I am so sorry, Patrizia. Things have not gone quite as well as I planned. I knew Louis had eyes everywhere, but I thought if I could just stay a step ahead, I..."

"Elise! What is wrong? What happened? Are you okay? Are Brianna and I in danger?"

"No, no, you are fine. I had a scare in Madrid. I felt like I was being followed. I started watching and going unusual places. The same two men would show up. I darted into a building to ditch my sweater, sling, and wig, then went out another exit and blended in with the crowd. I managed to lose them."

"That is good news!"

"Yes, but I am sure when I disappeared and they could not find me, they went back to retrace their steps, looking for me. I had no time to be careful. I am quite sure they found my wig and sling. It is possible they now know that it is not you they have been following in Europe."

Patrizia was trying to take it all in. "They still do not know it was you and they do not know where Brianna and I are. I do not understand why you are so upset?"

Elise hesitated. "The success of the plan rested on Louis thinking you were alone and in Europe. Now they will start over and expand their search. They will be looking for a mother and daughter, together."

"Even if they look in the United States, it is a big country. They will not find us," Patrizia said, but an uneasiness was spreading through her like cancer.

"Yes, it will be hard for them to find Brianna. She is young and will blend in with all the other American children, but..."

"What? Just say what you are thinking!"

"I'm so sorry, Patrizia! This was not supposed to happen! This is all my fault!"

"Tell me what you were going to say!"

Elise swallowed hard. "Now they will be looking for the two of you together. In America, you will stand out. Your stunning features and strong accent make you hard to forget."

"What should we do?" Patrizia said, her voice rising.

"Come back to France. Italian accents are not unusual here. With your changed hair style and clothing, you will be hard to find here."

"But what about Brianna?"

"Patrizia," Elise said, sounding defeated, "you must decide what you think is best. You know Louis will not stop looking for you. If he finds you, he will also find Brianna. If you leave her in America, she will be safer. You will be safer also. Without having to worry about Brianna, you have a better chance of eluding Louis or fighting him—if it comes to that."

"I cannot. I cannot leave her. What will I do?"

"You have to make a decision, but it does not have to be right now. Take a few days, or longer if needed, to think about it. I know you, Patrizia. You are a strong, bright, determined woman. You will figure out a way; when you do, call me at this number. We will help with the arrangements and make it happen."

When Patrizia hung up, she paced the floor. Her mind was racing. Grabbing a map, she climbed up on the bed and stared at it.

Brianna came over to the bed. "Up. I want up," she said, with outstretched hands.

Patrizia reached out to help her climb up. Brianna sat in her lap and they both stared at the map in front of them.

"I do not know what to do, my little one," she said. "Where do we go?" Overwhelmed by it all, she closed her eyes and began to pray silently. "Oh Lord, I do not know what to do. Where should I go? Do I take Brianna or leave her behind? Help me to know what to do and give me the strength to do what is best for Brianna. I do not care what happens to me, but please protect Brianna. Guide me in what I should do..."

Patrizia was so immersed in her prayer that she didn't even notice Brianna had turned around in her lap until she felt her little hands on her cheeks. When she opened her eyes, Brianna's smiling face was inches in front of her. In spite of the tension she was feeling, she laughed. "What is it, my darling?"

"Was Mama sleeping?"

"No, I was not sleeping. I was praying. I do not know what to do." She turned Brianna around and pointed to Ohio on the map. "This is where we are. I do not know where I should go."

Taking her chubby, wet thumb out of her mouth, Brianna pointed to the map. "Mitten," she said, pointing to a mitten surrounded by blue. Then she pointed to Lake Michigan. "Pretty."

Patrizia held her breath for a second. *Dear Lord*, she thought, *Are*

*you telling me I should go to Michigan? If not, you need to give me a
sign. This is all I have. I am taking this as your sign.*

To Brianna, she said, "It is pretty. I agree. We lived in a boot surrounded by water. Would you like to live in a mitten surrounded
by water?"

Brianna nodded her head emphatically.

"I should have known," Patrizia said, laughing. "You are leaving a
boot and moving to a mitten. Very well. Michigan it shall be."

Patrizia checked out at the desk. Not wanting anyone to know
she was going to Michigan, she mentioned heading for Kentucky.
She rented a car, crossed over from Ohio to Indiana and took
69 North up into Michigan, avoiding big cities like Detroit and
Chicago. Taking 96 West, she kept going until she was near Lake
Michigan, then took roads going north near the shoreline.

Her time with Brianna was bittersweet. She enjoyed spending
these last moments with her daughter, but realized more and more
that it was coming to an end. She was a target to Louis and keeping
Brianna with her was putting her in danger. She had to figure out
what to do. She couldn't go to the authorities. They would know
their identities and Brianna would end up with Louis.

Somehow, she had to find someone to leave her with that would
do what was best for Brianna. But how? More and more, she prayed.

Maybe she could find a couple to leave her with—maybe on their
doorstep. It sounded bizarre to leave a child on a doorstep like they
were nothing more than a package, but she didn't know what else
to do.

Patrizia spent days hunting for that perfect couple. She found
American culture stressful: her English, though fluent, had never
been tested immersively. She was getting depressed. She had never
realized how many married couples acted more like strangers
than two people in love. She could almost always guess accurately
which couples were married and which ones were dating. There
was a notable difference. The other thing that depressed her was
how many people acted impatient with their children, like they

were an annoyance. Patrizia began to wonder if that perfect couple even existed.

They were eating at Donna's Diner, a restaurant in a small town called Empire, when a young couple with a small boy came in and sat down at a table adjacent to them. The boy was telling his parents a story about something that had happened to him. They were listening intently to every word he said and started laughing. "You know, he has a point," the man said, smiling at his wife.

"He certainly does," she said.

Patrizia tried not to stare, but she kept looking over at the table and listened to every word being said. The couple seemed to enjoy each other's company, and they enjoyed the time they were spending with their son.

Patrizia studied them closely. He was tall and thin with light blond hair. She was of average height with long, straight, dishwater-blonde hair. They both seemed to have a relaxed, easygoing nature about them, which is what impressed Patrizia the most. She learned from eavesdropping that they were vacationing, and that their next stop was Point Betsie to see the lighthouse.

Patrizia looked at Brianna. The two of them had enjoyed the last few days they'd spent together. Brianna was more relaxed and was even sucking her thumb less often. It saddened Patrizia when she realized that Brianna had not once asked for her papa. A little girl should adore her papa, but Brianna was just as glad to be away from Louis as she was.

They left before the other family did. Patrizia looked at her map and found Point Betsie. It wasn't too far south of Empire. She drove her rental car there in silence. Brianna was babbling away and didn't even notice the tears her mama was crying. It had to be now. She knew they were about as perfect a couple as she would ever find. A life on the run and in hiding was not a good life for a child.

Patrizia parked the car a short distance down the road. She and Brianna walked together to the beach. The lighthouse was beautiful, rising proudly above the Lake Michigan shoreline. The waves were crashing against the breakers and sending sprays up into the air. There were too many people around the lighthouse. She took Brianna a little south of the lighthouse to a pile of rocks and busted-up cement she saw. Brianna was looking at the seagulls and the water. She was delighted by it all.

Almost fifteen minutes later, Patrizia saw the family arrive. She scribbled a note on a piece of paper and placed Brianna next to the rocks. "Brianna. We are going to play a game. Can you hide here and be quiet?"

Brianna nodded her head, 'yes.'

"That's my good girl. Do not move." Patrizia saw a young boy. "Could you give this note to that couple over there?"

"Give it to them yourself," he said.

Patrizia grimaced. "Here is five dollars if you will give this note to them."

He took the money and the note.

Scurrying up the bank and hiding behind an old lifesaving station, she watched. The couple took the note and read it. Running over to the rocks, they looked around. Seeing no one, they tried to pick Brianna up, but she began wailing.

Patrizia turned and raced for the car, trying to outrun the cries of "Mama!" that reached her. She got in and sped away while sobbing and continually wiping away tears with her sleeve. With a white-knuckled grip on the steering wheel, she cursed Louis with a steady stream of Italian words.

Pushing to put distance between herself and Point Betsie, she drove until she was unable to drive any more. Finding an almost-empty rest stop, she broke down, crying and trying to gulp in air as she rocked back and forth, hugging herself.

"Brianna. My baby. My sweet, sweet baby," were the repeated words. "Oh God, why did all this have to happen? She must be terrified. Please protect her and be with her!"

Praying. Cursing. Crying. She began to drive again, not stopping until Grand Rapids. There, she checked into a room. Alone. She again cursed Louis for doing this to them.

The next morning, Patrizia went down to the counter to check out. She overheard some people talking. "Did you hear the news last night? A baby was found up by the Sleeping Bear Dunes, abandoned. Can you believe that? They are trying to find out if anyone knows who her parents are."

"What kind of parents would just leave their kid like that?" was the response. "The poor child. What is the world coming to?"

Patrizia tried to hide the guilt and shame she was feeling. How could she expect anyone to understand? She didn't even understand it herself. Nothing in her life had turned out at all the way she'd planned it. The only comfort she had was that she knew Brianna was in good hands; the couple had done the right thing and notified the authorities immediately. If they were unable to raise Brianna, or if they did not want her, the government would see that she was placed in a good home. "Please, God," she said silently. "Watch over my little Brianna. Give her a good home."

CHAPTER TEN

The trip back to France was the longest trip of her life. The further away she got, the bigger the empty hole in her heart became. She never would have gotten through it if it weren't for Elise. She was there with Patrizia, helping her through it all.

Patrizia spent the next six years working in little shops in France under an assumed name. They had been successful in eluding Louis, but Patrizia eventually made one fatal mistake. She heard through Elise that her father was in the hospital and not expected to live much longer. He had been fighting a cancer that rapidly spread through his body, but he was losing the battle. She knew her disappearance had caused him grief. If anyone understood the broken heart of a parent separated from their child, it was her. She decided she would go to Italy and sneak in to see him. Her success for six years in hiding from Louis gave her false confidence that she could pull it off.

Patrizia felt excited as she drove through Italy. The sculptures and beautiful scenery brought back memories from her childhood. As she was growing up, she had taken the statuary and architecture for granted, but now she appreciated their beauty. She began to realize just how much she missed Italy. Even being able to speak her native tongue was a thrill.

She drove straight to the hospital and went up to the fifth floor, waiting for a moment when there were no visitors in his room. She stood next to her father's bedside and was horrified at how small and frail he looked. He was sleeping, but his breathing was labored. She took his hand in hers and started to pat it. "Papa," she whispered. "Papa, it is me, Patrizia."

Slowly his eyes opened. He stared at her in disbelief. He smiled, but could not talk because of the tubes. Tears were streaming down his cheeks. He gave her hand a squeeze.

"It is okay, Papa. Do not cry. I am here now. I am fine, and Brianna is safe."

He gave a weak nod.

When Patrizia's mama came into the room, they both began crying and hugging each other. "Patrizia, we never thought we would see you again."

"Oh Mama, I am so sorry. I know I caused you and Papa much pain, but I cannot stay. I will have to go back immediately, and we must not let anyone know I was here."

"Yes, yes. We will be very careful."

Patrizia stayed by her papa's bedside a while longer, then left before her siblings returned. She told her mama goodbye and left the hospital. She would not be able to stay until the end or attend the funeral, but at least she'd gotten to tell him one final time how much she loved him.

In a daze, Patrizia walked out to the parking lot. It had been emotionally draining, and many thoughts occupied her. She didn't even notice the footsteps coming up behind her.

A hand clasped over her mouth and a strong arm jerked her back tightly against a muscled body, crushing her painfully. Fighting with all her might to get free didn't faze her captor. He laughed in her ear.

Louis. Overcome by renewed panic, her muffled screams and futile attempts to break free gained her nothing.

"You were not expecting me? You thought you could just come back to Italy and I would not find out?"

He removed his hand.

"Louis, you are hurting me. Please let me go."

"Hurting you? You will soon know what it means to hurt," he said, dragging her towards his car.

Patrizia yelled and screamed. People in the parking lot began to gather as she twisted, trying to escape.

"Eh!" a young man yelled, stepping forward. "Let go of her!"

"Stay out of this. This is not your concern," Louis said.

"I am afraid it is. Let go of her now," he said as he walked towards them.

Louis pulled out a gun and fired a couple shots. Screams came from the crowd as they panicked and fled. A nearby officer came running. "Drop the gun! Drop the gun!" he yelled. Louis hesitated, but reluctantly complied. As they took him away he yelled viciously at Patrizia, swearing to someday have revenge. He never showed remorse for, or even glanced at, the young man dying on the pavement.

Patrizia shook uncontrollably. When the medics arrived, they gave her a sedative to calm her down. The police took her to the station to get a statement. While she was there she called Elise's father for advice.

"Leave the country immediately," he said.

"But I cannot. They want me to testify at the trial."

"It sounds like they have plenty of witnesses. They do not need you. You must realize it will come out in the trial that you abandoned your daughter. You could go to jail if you refuse to tell them where she is."

"I see. That never entered my thoughts." Upon ending the conversation, she hung up the phone and left Italy for the last time.

CHAPTER ELEVEN

The next 15 years were a struggle. Patrizia worked hard in a futile attempt to chase thoughts of Brianna away. Remembering hurt too much, and she ached to hold the daughter that had been her whole life. Just about everything reminded her of Brianna. Many nights she would wake up with her pillow damp from tears, her daughter's cries haunting her.

Clinging to her belief that God was looking out for them, she faithfully prayed for Brianna every night.

She made friends and had a social life, but never got involved with anyone. Not that men didn't try. Her aloofness made her that much more intriguing to some, but she was not about to endanger anyone else. Enough people had been hurt already because of her mistakes. Now, Louis would be getting out of prison soon.

Patrizia glanced at the mail on the table. Rifling through the stack of envelopes, her eyes froze on one postmarked from the United States. An uneasy feeling settled upon her. She only knew one person from America.

With shaky hands, she opened it. Printed on plain paper were the words:

Where could Brianna be?
Meet me at the lighthouse—
You know which one.
May 19, 7:00 p.m.
Who will find her first?

"Louis! Damn you!" Patrizia said, shouting and pounding the heel of her hand sharply on the table. She paced back and forth, biting her nails. Now there was no doubt Louis knew where she was; furthermore, he clearly wouldn't be content to leave Brianna out of whatever he had planned.

For all she knew, someone could be outside her apartment right now, watching her. She nervously looked out the window, then grabbed the phone.

"Bonjour, Patrizia. How are you?"

"Elise, I need your help."

"Is it something that can wait? I have a meeting in ten minutes."

"No...please...now."

Elise frowned into her phone. Demanding was not a normal characteristic of Patrizia.

"It is Louis, no?"

"Yes," she said, barely speaking.

"I will be on my way immediately."

Thirty minutes later Elise rushed through the door. She ran to Patrizia and hugged her sobbing friend.

"What is going on? You must tell me."

Patrizia handed over the terse letter.

Elise read the note and dropped it on the table. "But how? He is still in Italy. The rat. He must have had someone mail it for him. Perfect alibi. Hard for us to accuse a man in an Italian prison of sending a letter from America. He would say we were framing him. What are you going to do?"

"I have to go."

"No, you must not. He will kill you."

"I have no choice."

"I still cannot believe they are letting him out this early. Only fifteen years for killing a man? Something is not right about all of this."

"I agree. He has somehow used his connections."

"You cannot go, Patrizia! He has learned nothing and will not stop until he has destroyed you."

"I know, but Brianna...every day I have prayed for twenty years that she would be kept safe. God has been faithful. I must trust he will continue to protect us."

Elise knew she could not talk her out of it.

"Why did I ever get involved with him?"

"Do not berate yourself. You were young and impressionable. Louis came around, promising you the world, even wanted to claim Brianna as his own. Who would not have fallen for his charm?"

"Yes, he was wonderful. After we were married, everything gradually changed...it was bad enough when he would beat me, but when he started losing his patience with Brianna and leaving bruises on her, I knew I had to do something. I could not bear to see the cowering child she was becoming."

"You did the right thing. I will come with you."

"No. Twenty years ago, you put yourself in danger helping me. Not this time. I will do this alone."

"I enjoyed disguising myself as you and using Louis's charge cards to travel around Europe while you and Brianna escaped to America. Making him the fool was the greatest fun...a true shame his men caught up so quickly."

"You are a wonderful friend. Thank you, but I must do this alone."

Elise sighed as they busied themselves making arrangements for the flight. The next day they hugged each other and said their tearful goodbyes.

When Patrizia arrived in Michigan, she had no problem renting a small cabin across the road from Crystal Lake. It was the middle of May and the peak tourism season had not yet started. She was only a short drive away from Point Betsie. Tomorrow was the night she would have to go to the lighthouse and meet the anonymous writer of the note.

Going to bed that night was a waste of time. Not knowing if harm was waiting for her out at Point Betsie, she didn't get one minute of sleep. Maybe if she cooperated, Louis would leave Brianna out of it? After all, it was her that he was angry with, not Brianna.

It was raining and the sky was already dark when Patrizia reached the lighthouse. She parked her car and stared out over the lake. The dark, stormy sky looked foreboding. She hoped it wasn't an omen.

Patrizia had chosen to wear a dress. From the note, it didn't sound like they had found Brianna, but Louis was a master of deception. She could already be in danger. For all she knew Brianna might be waiting for her there, her head filled up with Louis's lies. Foolishly, she was worried about the impression Brianna would form of her. She wrapped her sweater tightly around her. An umbrella and a rain coat would have been nice, but she wasn't thinking straight when she left. Taking a deep breath, she stepped out of the safety of the rented vehicle.

Before hitting the beach, she glanced around, occasionally looking over her shoulder. She didn't like surprises. Taking off her sand-filled shoes, she held them in her hand. It was dark, broken up only by the fleeting light from the lighthouse. The tall, cold structure looked eerie with its beam cutting the sky, making her feel tiny and insignificant.

The wind blew hard pellets of rain against her skin. Angry, crashing waves and clapping thunder snuffed out any other sounds of the night. She wished it would all go away. Seeing no one, she wondered if he would come. Her clothes were soaked and clung to her like plastic wrap on cheese. Patrizia was shivering. The waves continuously came up on the shore toward her, like fingers stretching out to grab her, before melting slowly away.

Turning, she saw a man casually walking in her direction. He was of average height, but had broad shoulders and wore a navy hooded jacket. He had to be the one she was supposed to meet: who else would be out on a night like this? She stood there, vulnerable, half expecting him to pull out a gun and shoot her, just like a scene in a bad movie. But she knew that wasn't Louis's style. No, he would want to see her suffer first.

She went out to meet him. "Who are you, and what do you want?"

"Who I am isn't important. Louis is anxious to see you again."

"I am sure he is, but why did I have to come all the way over here? He could have met with me in France."

The man grinned. "I hear you're good at disappearing. He's not taking any chances you'll take off again."

"Why is this meeting any different? I could take off right now if I wanted."

"I think you know the answer to that. Brianna is here."

"Where?"

"In the area. I haven't found her yet, but I will."

"In Frankfort?"

He laughed. "If I told you that, you would know as much as I do. I like having a head start. We'll see who can find her first."

"Who will find her first?" she asked, incredulously. "This is not some stupid game! Do you realize how dangerous Louis is?"

"I'm not afraid of him."

"Not afraid?" Her nerves shot, Patrizia began to laugh hysterically. "I cannot believe I am standing here in a storm talking to an idiot like you. Go back to wherever you slithered from." She turned to leave.

"Wait," he yelled over the sound of the crashing waves. "I can't let you leave."

"You have no choice. Are you going to shoot me? No. Louis would not like you stealing his fun."

"I don't have to worry about Louis, because you're coming with me. No more disappearing acts."

"You found me once. You will have to find me again."

He stepped toward her, grabbing her shoulders. "You think you're smart, don't you? I'm losing my patience."

"I'm not coming with you. You tell Louis I will talk to him and only him, but I am not wasting my time with you."

He grabbed a fistful of her bulky sweater and pulled her closer, slowly stroking her cheek with his other hand. "You're coming with me," he said, flashing a menacing grin.

Panicking, Patrizia screamed, bending and twisting. When his grip loosened, she bent down and stepped backwards until she slipped out of the sweater.

He stood surprised, with sweater in hand. Patrizia fled towards her vehicle. He was right behind her. *No time. Keep running.* His shoes, wet and sandy, slowed him down. She ran down the road toward the main highway like a deer on opening day. Blinded by fright and with rain streaming down her face, she didn't see the Camaro coming around the curve. Running out in front of it and tumbling forward, she fell. As she scrambled to get back up, she heard a horn honking, then a voice yelling, but they seemed to be far, far away. She kept running as if demons from hell were hot on her heels.

The man in pursuit hid behind a tree so the driver couldn't see him. A woman got out of the car to chase after Patrizia. He followed, making sure to stay out of sight. The woman turned suddenly to go back to her vehicle. As he darted behind a tree, lightning flashed across the sky. The eyes he was staring into were the same big, scared brown eyes he had seen seconds before: Patrizia's eyes, but framed in a slightly different, younger face. Her wet hair clung to her head, emphasizing the similarity of their features. Could he be this lucky? Was this woman the one he had been looking for? He quickly stepped back into the darkness. He would follow. He had to find out who she was.

WRATH OF THE MANITOU

CHAPTER TWELVE

A couple days had passed since Bree first met with her father Louis. Because of their work schedules, this was the first chance Bree and Denver had to see each other. She left the door unlocked for him, so he knocked and came on in.

"Hello," he said, "anybody home?"

"In here," she answered. She came out to greet him with a kiss, and then he followed her into the kitchen.

"I was just getting myself an apple," she said, as she reached into the refrigerator. "Want one?"

"Sure."

Bree took an apple out and tossed it in Denver's direction. He snatched it out of the air with one hand.

"Good catch."

"Not as good as this one," he said, setting the apple down and grabbing her as she walked by. Bree laughed as he spun her around and plopped her down on his lap.

"I've been thinking about you all day," Denver continued, taking on a somber tone. "I was wondering how you were doing with everything that's just happened. Are you okay?"

She wrapped her arm around his neck, slowly shook her head, and let out a heavy sigh. "I don't even know how to begin to describe how I feel. The last two nights I could barely sleep. My mind was in overdrive, thinking about the same things over and over again.

The pictures of my grandparents, my mother, and cousins—I keep seeing them in my mind and imagining what they're like. And of course, there's Louis. I just -"

Bree stopped for a moment, trying to fight the tears, but it was no use. Soon she was sobbing. Denver wrapped his arms around her and Bree buried her face on his shoulder. Denver gently rocked her and let her cry. "It's okay," he kept whispering softly in her ear. "It's okay."

Bree clung to him, finding solace and comfort in his arms. "I can't believe," she said between sobs, "that my father's been looking for me all these years. All this time I thought he didn't want me, when the truth is he never stopped looking for me. My heart feels like it can't contain everything, like it's going to burst. I feel happiness and joy, but I also feel sorrow for all the heartache he must have gone through and all the lost years that we could have spent together. It's just so much to deal with. The explanations I had worked up in my mind don't even come close to what really happened."

When the tears finally stopped flowing, Bree got up, grabbing a box of tissues on their way to the living room to sit on the couch.

"I don't know why I thought about my birth parents so much when I was growing up. I had a loving home with parents who truly cared about me. That's more than what a lot of people have. I should have been happy, but somehow, I always felt deep down that there must be something wrong with me. I saw how much all my friends' parents loved and cared for them, but my birth parents just left me and never looked back—at least, that's what I always thought. I believed they never cared at all whether they saw me again. I mean, how hard could it be to find me if they one day decided to look for me? It's not like I had a closed adoption. My abandonment was in every paper in this area, along with the name of the family that found me. All they had to do was look."

"I was telling Grandmother about you being found out at Point Betsie," Denver said. "She said she could remember hearing about that years ago. It was quite a big deal to have something like that happen in this little community. Everyone was in an uproar, and there were people all over the area wanting to adopt you. You were quite popular," he added, teasing her.

"You didn't realize you were dating a celebrity, did you?"

"No, I didn't. I've got a real Italian beauty on my hands. Sophia Loren has nothing on you."

Bree laughed. It felt so good to know something about her roots. Now when anyone asked what her ethnicity was, she could answer instead of feeling uncomfortable and dodging the subject. She smiled as she thought about it.

"Someday I'll have lots of little kids. I'll make spaghetti and bake garlic bread."

"Spaghetti with lots of spicy meatsaballas," Denver embellished.

"Of course! What kind of mama would I be if I couldn't make spaghetti with spicy meatsaballas?"

"A sexy one," he said, nibbling on her ear. "I see you in an apron—and nothing else."

"You're terrible!" she said, elbowing him and laughing. "How could I walk around in just an apron? What about Junior and all the others?"

"I sent them off to their grandmama's."

"Oh, I see what kind of father you're going to be."

"One who adores their mama," he said as he kissed her neck, and then started tickling her. Bree squirmed around and started tickling him back. They wrestled around and ended up snuggled together.

They both settled down, deep in their own thoughts. Denver pulled her even closer to him, unable to get close enough. He could lose himself in the smell of her hair and the softness of her skin. Tonight, she had seemed so vulnerable that it made him want to protect her and shield her from all harm. He was happy for her and didn't want to spoil anything, but the eyes of the woman in the photograph kept haunting him. Could she have really left her child? There were just too many holes in Louis's story. He tried to shake the disturbing thoughts that kept creeping into his mind.

It didn't help that Grandmother kept warning him to be careful. Even when she didn't say a word, he could see the anxiety in her face.

He wanted to bring it up again with Bree, but the last time he did she'd gotten upset and distant with him. He didn't want to lose her. That was one thing of which he was certain.

Denver finally broke the silence by asking one of the many questions running through his mind. "Have you told your parents yet?"

Bree bristled a little when she heard the question. "No. I know I should, but I've been dreading it. I don't want them to think they're being replaced or feel like they're losing me."

"I'm sure they'll understand, but if you're worried about what they'll think, why don't you invite them up this weekend for dinner? The Fourth of July would be a great time to come. It's a holiday, and it will let them know they're still important to you and that you miss them."

Bree sat up. "That's a great idea! I've been wanting to ask them up anyway. You're a genius!"

"I know," he said, feigning humility. "It's a gift of mine."

Bree rolled her eyes. "Oh, brother! No more compliments for you."

Denver laughed and brought her back to the subject. "Why don't you call them now and get it over with?"

She hesitated, but only for a minute. "I think I will."

Bree went out to get her cell phone and brought it in with her to the living room, where she sat down in the big armchair. She had baggy jeans and a baggy T-shirt on, but it didn't disguise her feminine figure.

Denver watched her as she pulled her legs up and tucked her feet under her. She gave her head a little toss to get her hair away from her face. As she dialed she gave Denver a nervous smile. Somehow it made him melt inside, and he knew without a doubt that there would be no one for him but her.

When Bree started talking to her mother on the phone, Denver wondered if he should go out into the kitchen to give her some privacy, but the glances she kept giving him told him otherwise. She seemed to need and want him there, and it made him feel good.

"...Mom," Bree said, her voice sounding shaky. "I did call tonight for a specific reason. I have something I have to tell you. I've put it off for a couple days now, because it's been so hard to work up the courage. I don't want you or Dad to be upset.

"...No. Nothing's wrong. I'm okay. I just wanted to let you know that I met someone last Saturday..."

Bree laughed. "No, it's not a guy. Well, I mean—yes, it is a guy, but not that kind of guy..."

She took a deep breath and grimaced before saying the words: "I met my birth father."

Bree was silent for a moment. "Mom? Are you still there?...Yes. My birth father," she said, tilting her head down and sniffling. "...No, I wasn't looking for him. *He* found *me*. He's been looking for me all these years.

"...His name is Louis Cipriano. He has an Italian accent and calls me his little Brianna.

"...Yes, it's been very emotional. I didn't think I would ever meet him. He showed me pictures of my birth mother. Oh Mom, please don't cry," she said, disobeying her own orders.

Bree closed her eyes and nodded her head as tears streamed down her cheeks. Denver grabbed the box of tissues and handed them to her. He had a good idea of what was being said on the other end of the line.

"...No one could take your place. You will always be my mom. All my memories are of you, Dad, and Steven. You're my family.

"...Yes, put him on. Dad?...I'm fine. How are you?...I met him Saturday. Yes, I'm sure it's him. He showed me pictures of me with him and my mother. I look just like her...No, I haven't met her and I don't think I'm going to."

Bree continued to tell him about everything that had happened before having to abruptly end the conversation.

"...I'll always be your girl...I love you too, Dad." Those were the last words Bree could manage to get out before losing control.

Before he knew what was happening, Bree was handing Denver the phone. She was crying too hard to finish talking. Denver's eyes grew wide and he gave her a look, questioning her. He had never met or talked to her parents before. He was not expecting to have to talk to them at such a personal and trying time. She nodded for him to take it.

He hesitantly accepted it. "Hello," he said. He introduced himself to Mr. Darby as Bree's friend Denver. He convinced him that Bree was fine, but she couldn't finish talking at the moment. He relayed to Mr. Darby that Bree wanted to invite them up for dinner that coming weekend.

Mr. Darby told Denver they would leave to come up Saturday morning, and that he was looking forward to meeting him.

Denver said goodbye and hung up the phone. He sat there watching Bree. She looked so small, curled up into a ball in that big chair with her arms wrapped around her knees. The puffy eyes and tear-stained face didn't help much either.

"Come here," he whispered softly, motioning to the spot next to him on the couch. She walked over and he held out his arms for her to snuggle up into.

"I'm sorry, Denver. I didn't mean to put you in an awkward position like that."

"It's okay. I'm glad I was here to help."

"I think that was the hardest thing I've had to do in my whole life. If you weren't here, I would have kept putting it off and worrying about it. It's good to have it over with."

Bree was emotionally drained and felt beat. She lay against Denver with her head on his chest. They talked for a while, with Bree's voice getting softer and quieter as the minutes passed. Soon she was sound asleep.

Denver sat there for half an hour just letting her sleep before disentangling himself. He went into her room to turn the sheets and blanket down. When he picked her up to carry her into her room, she opened her eyelids just for a moment.

"Denver," she said softly; then, she was sleeping again.

He laid her down on the bed and pulled just the sheet over her. It was the end of June, and warm enough in her little apartment. He looked at her long, dark lashes resting against her cheeks and the chocolate-brown hair spread against the white pillowcase. Walking away was so hard to do when what he really wanted was to crawl into the bed with her.

He turned all the lights in the apartment off, and double-checked the door to make sure it was locked before stepping outside.

When Bree first woke up the next morning, she was confused. She still had her jeans and T-shirt on, but could not remember how she'd gotten into her room. Slowly it came back to her, and she vaguely remembered Denver carrying her. She got up to look for him but he wasn't there. All she found was a note saying he would see her tomorrow.

The idea of Denver carrying her into her bedroom and lying her down on the bed sent warm and arousing desires through her. She wished she could remember it more clearly.

Bree glanced up at the clock on the wall. It was 10:00 am. She could not believe she'd slept almost twelve hours. It was a good thing she wasn't supposed to meet Louis for lunch until one o'clock. It gave her plenty of time to relax, clean up her apartment, and get ready. They had agreed to meet at the restaurant instead of him picking her up. Bree thought it was ridiculous, but she had promised Denver she would only meet Louis in public places.

Over lunch they talked about everything. Louis spoke of Italy and his life growing up there, the beautiful mountains, the harbors and beaches. He also spoke of the culture of his country, the museums, and the art. It made Bree long to see it. Someday, she promised herself, she would go there.

At his insistence, Bree told Louis all she could about her childhood. She talked about her brother Steven and her parents. She told him about playing Little League softball as a young girl, and taking dance and singing lessons. Music was a passion of hers. In high school, the drama club had put on a play and she'd had a singing role in it.

At last she told him how she had always wondered about her birth parents, but had never had the courage to look for them because she didn't want to hurt her mom and dad.

He seemed to understand and respect her loyalty to them. "It is admirable that you give them the respect they deserve. They have raised you well. I was so afraid of how you were being treated. I was not even sure if you were still alive. I feel blessed that we have been reunited, and that all my fears were for nothing."

Bree left the restaurant that afternoon in good spirits, which was much better than yesterday when all she seemed able to do was cry. She headed back to her apartment to change before leaving for work.

When she arrived at work, the Lakeshore Bar was hopping. The dinner crowd had every table occupied, and there were those waiting in line to be seated. It was the week before the Fourth of July and tourists had invaded the area, which was good for everyone. Most of the local merchants needed the money they made in the summer to carry them through the winter. Larry was pleased with the business they were getting and was kept occupied with drink orders.

Bree was in high spirits also, joking around with the customers and raking in big tips. Nothing, she was sure, would rattle her today. She buzzed around as quickly as she could, taking and serving orders and clearing tables.

"Oh, miss," a voice said to Bree as she walked by. She stopped to see who had called her. The smile she wore quickly left her face.

"What do you want?" she asked, glaring into the smug, smiling face of Scott Proctor.

"A menu and a beer would do for beginners."

She gave him an artificial smile and answered sweetly, "I would love to help you, sir, but you're not at my table. I'll send Sheila right over."

As she walked away she could hear him laughing. It irritated her but she kept on walking, pretending she didn't hear him. She wasn't going to give him the satisfaction of knowing he could get to her.

Bree kept busy working, and she intentionally avoided looking in his direction. She even went around the next table over to avoid walking past him. Her plan was working and she was feeling quite pleased with herself, until she went up to one of her tables and found him sitting there, that same obnoxious grin on his face.

Bree put her hand on her hip and stared him in the eye. "What are you doing at my table?"

He grinned broadly. "I didn't like the view at the other one, so when a table opened up I took it. It's much better over here. Redheads are nice, but I prefer brunettes," he said, looking her over.

"Lucky me," she said. "What would you like to drink, sir?" She spoke in a cold, all-business voice, ignoring his comment.

"Oh please, Brianna, call me Scott. I'd like to think we're friends," he said, oozing with charm.

"What gave you that idea?"

"If you've forgotten, I did help get you together with your father. You owe it to me to at least be civil."

"I'm sure Louis paid you well, so I owe you nothing," she said, and then got back to business. "If I remember correctly, you wanted a beer. Here is your menu," she said, then added before she walked away, "sir."

When she came back with his beer, she asked him if he was ready to order. He said yes, but kept looking over the menu. Bree waited impatiently.

"I'm a meat-and-potatoes kind of guy. I'll have the steak special," he said, closing up the menu and handing it to her. "Medium. I like it a little juicy. How about you? How do you like it, Brianna?"

Bree glared at him in disbelief, her face burning red with rage barely under control. She stormed away from the table, almost knocking a customer over, and pushed open the door to the kitchen.

Sheila had seen Bree go back there and followed her. Bree was pacing back and forth, muttering to herself. At the end of the counter her order pad lay where she had flung it.

"I can't believe it! I can't believe it!" Bree said, seething with rage. "That man—oh!" she said, stomping her foot.

"Honey, what did he say to you?" Sheila asked, trying to calm her down.

Bree told her word for word, and Sheila was incensed. "I'll tell Larry and he'll have him thrown out of here in a second."

"No. We can't do that. This place is packed, and I haven't seen Larry happier. If we cause a scene, it won't be good for business. I just need a moment to calm down. It's part of my job to put up with creeps like him."

"No," Sheila said, disagreeing. "We never have to put up with that."

Sheila looked closely at Bree. She was so wound up, she half-expected to see her shoot through the air across the room.

"Why don't you let me take care of it?" Sheila suggested. "I've been doing this long enough that I've heard everything by now. I know exactly how to handle his kind."

"Thanks so much. I just can't deal with him right now."

"No sweat. It's no problem at all."

"I owe you one."

"You sure do," Sheila said, kidding her as she went back out through the kitchen door.

When Scott's order was ready, Sheila brought it out to him. "What happened to my waitress?" he demanded.

"There's been a change in table assignments. This one's mine."

"Well, maybe I'll have to find another table again."

"And maybe we'll just switch tables again. You're stuck with me, or you can leave. It's up to you."

Scott grinned. If they thought he could be so easily discouraged, they were wrong. "I think I'll stay. Oh, by the way, is it true what they say about redheads?" he asked, whispering an obscene question to her.

Sheila was disgusted, but her face didn't betray her. She wasn't about to give him the satisfaction. "That and more," she answered seductively, leaning forward, "but you'll just have to take my word for it honey, 'cause you'll never find out."

Sheila walked away slowly, swinging her hips like she normally did, just to let him know he had not affected her in the least.

Scott chewed his food slowly and ordered another beer every now and then. All night he kept eyeing Bree; even though she never looked his way, she could feel his eyes on her. It made her jittery, and once she even dropped a glass and broke it. Scott grinned with satisfaction. Every once in a while he would test Sheila, but he never got the reaction he wanted. She was a tough one.

The next time Bree and Sheila were back in the kitchen together, Sheila told Bree some of the things he'd said to her.

"It's hard to believe," Sheila said, shaking her head, "that God would wrap a jackass like him in such a nice package. I can't believe some of the raunchy lines he used on me. The dinner crowd is leaving and it's clearing out a bit. If he doesn't leave soon, I'll have Larry toss him out. I'm growing tired of him."

As luck would have it, it didn't come to that. Scott finally left on his own, and Bree and Sheila couldn't have been happier.

Around ten o'clock Denver came in, and Bree took her break so she could talk to him. Sheila came over to wait on them.

"Hi, Denver. What can I get you?"

"I'll just have a Coke."

"Boy," she said, "we could have used you in here about half an hour ago."

Bree was trying to motion to her to stop, but it was too late.

"Why? What happened?"

Sheila caught the look on Bree's face and realized she had made a mistake.

"It wasn't that big of a deal," she said, trying to downplay it. "Just some guy being a jerk. We get one of those every now and then." Sheila quickly turned to make her escape.

Denver turned to Bree to get more information about what had happened. She hadn't planned on telling him, but since he asked she didn't have a choice. She couldn't lie to him.

Denver insisted on staying until closing to follow her home. He walked with her to the door and made sure no one was inside.

"You will call me if he shows up again tomorrow, won't you?"

"I feel pretty safe as long as I'm inside and Larry and everyone else is there, but if it'll make you feel better I will."

"It would. Anyone who treats women the way he does isn't someone to be taken lightly. I don't trust him."

Bree agreed. She didn't trust him either. After they said goodbye, Denver waited outside her door until he heard the click of the deadbolt.

The next night, Bree and Sheila were relieved when Scott failed to show up. The dinner crowd came and went without any sign of him, but their reprieve didn't last long. Around eight thirty he came strolling in and sat down at a back table.

"I told Denver I'd call him if he showed up," Bree said to Sheila, "but that might make things worse."

"I think you should call. When a creep like him keeps coming back, they're looking for trouble. He won't quit until he gets it. I don't think it would hurt for him to know you have someone looking out for you."

"Maybe you're right. I'll make that call," Bree said, and pulled out her cell phone.

Charlie was just coming in the door. "Hey, Bree, what's up?"

"Oh, hi, Charlie," she said half-heartedly and continued on by.

"What's the matter with her?" he asked Sheila.

"The bad penny has returned. Back table. He was here last night harassing both of us. I've been able to handle it, but he won't lay off Bree. He seems to enjoy shaking her up."

"I'll keep an eye on him," he said, openly staring in the direction of the back table. "I think that's the same guy Larry had to talk to before."

When Scott saw they were looking in his direction and talking about him, he smiled and waved.

"Well, he's a regular old smartass, isn't he?" Charlie said, unamused. "I halfway hope he gives me a reason to haul him away."

"He's a real charmer, isn't he?" Sheila asked, smirking as she walked off.

About twenty minutes had passed before Denver walked into the bar. He paused in the doorway as he surveyed the room.

Bree spotted him first. He looked so serious with that hawk-like expression on his face. He had on gray dress-casual pants and a navy short-sleeved shirt.

Bree smiled and let out a sigh of relief—until then she hadn't realized just how tense she was. She walked over to the door and gave him a quick kiss.

"Is everything okay?"

"Yes," she said, nodding her head. "Sheila's been nice enough to take his table again, so I've been able to avoid him."

"I'm assuming Scott's the guy at the back table, sitting by himself," he said, without looking in that direction.

Bree nodded her affirmation. "Please don't start anything, Denver. I don't want any trouble if it can be avoided. He hasn't said anything to me yet tonight, and as long as he leaves me alone, I'll be happy."

"I don't want any trouble either. Nothing would make me happier than him walking out that door right now and us never seeing him again, but I'm afraid that's not up to me. It's his move, and I hate waiting to see what he's going to do."

"I know," she said, slipping her arm through his as they walked over to the bar. Denver took a seat next to Charlie; from there he could see everything Scott was doing reflected in the mirror on the wall behind the bar.

Bree brought Denver a Coke and talked to him whenever she could spare a minute. Denver and Sheila told Larry and Charlie everything that had been going on.

After a while, Scott got up and went over to another table to talk to some ladies sitting there. They seemed to welcome his company and were enjoying talking to him. After putting away a few more beers, however, they became less impressed.

His laughter grew louder and his speech slurred. If Bree walked anywhere in his range of vision, he openly leered at her. The ladies soon left.

Denver was seething under his calm exterior.

"Waitress, waitress," Scott called out. "Hey, Red, bring me another brewski."

"In a minute," Sheila answered as she finished taking care of her other customers.

Scott sat there sulking. He didn't like being ignored, so he turned his attention elsewhere. "Oh, Brianna," he said, "come here, Brianna."

"Just ignore him, honey," Sheila said. "I'll get to him when I can. He has to wait like everyone else does."

Bree nodded and continued to clear her tables.

"Ohhhh, Briannnna," he said, laughing loudly. "Come to Scotty. Scotty wants you," he continued, starting to laugh hysterically, slapping the table.

He started to get up out of his seat, but fell back into it.

At this point, Denver had taken all he could take. He got off his stool and took his glass over to Scott's table, sitting in the chair next to him. He twirled the ice around in his glass, not saying a word.

"What's he doing?" Bree asked Charlie and started to walk towards the table.

Charlie reached out and grabbed her arm. "Let Denver handle it, Bree. You know I'll back him up if it comes to that."

"I know," she said, feeling frustrated but listening to his advice. "I just don't want him getting hurt or in trouble because of me."

They saw Scott turn to Denver and talk to him. "I don't remember saying you could sit there," he said, in his slurred speech.

Denver sat there calmly, took a drink, and crunched on an ice cube. When he was ready, he answered, "I don't remember asking for your permission."

"Ewww," Scott answered. "Is lover boy jealous of his girlfriend? I can't say as I blame ya. With looks like that and a body to go with it, I'd..."

"If you don't leave Bree alone," Denver cut in through clenched teeth, "you'll be dealing with me."

"Maybe I'll leave her alone," Scott said, shrugging his shoulders, "but then again, maybe I won't."

Denver stood up. "If you're having trouble deciding, we can take it outside right now and I can help you make up your mind."

Scott stood up, grabbing the table with one hand to steady himself. "I think I'll stay inside. Now, it'd be different if Brianna offered to go outside with me, I would..."

Denver didn't wait to hear what he had to say. He knew he had to walk away before he lost control, but as he did he intentionally brushed into Scott with his shoulder.

Scott staggered a little but regained his footing. "Hey!" he yelled, following Denver. "You can't push me around like that and walk away." He came up behind Denver and gave him a shove. "Hey! I'm talking to you."

Without saying a word, Denver spun around and punched him on the chin. Scott went reeling backwards, crashing into a table and slumping down to the floor. Scott moaned a little and slowly sat up. He rubbed his chin. There was blood on it. He had a fat, bloody lip.

Anger flashed in his eyes, and Denver stood there waiting for him to get up.

When he finally rose to his feet, Scott started walking towards Denver, but Charlie quickly stepped between them, intervening.

"Just cool it," Charlie said to Scott.

Scott glared at him. "I want someone to call the police. He assaulted me and I'm pressing charges."

Bree had come over to stand by Denver's side, and Charlie glanced at them with a sly grin. He turned back to Scott and took out his badge. "At your service, and I didn't see a thing. Did you?"

he asked Denver and Bree. They each shook their head 'no.' "Hey Larry," he yelled over toward the bar. "Did you see anything?"

"No, nothing," he said, shaking his head and faking a puzzled look.

Scott looked into the face of each person, turning slowly around. He knew he had been beat.

Denver and Bree began to walk away.

"Hey! Geronimo! I'm talking to you!" Scott yelled, pointing at Denver.

Denver looked back and glared at him, but chose not to be baited.

"You're gonna pay for this! All of you are going to pay!" Scott shouted before staggering out the door.

Bree shivered and Denver put a protective arm around her.

"Hey," Sheila said, "speaking of paying for things...he didn't pay his bill."

"I'll get it," Denver said, throwing money on the table. "The sooner he's gone, the better."

"I'll call the station and tell them to send a car," Charlie said to Larry as he headed toward the door, grinning with satisfaction. "I don't think that boy should be driving in his condition. A night in the slammer to cool off might do him some good."

CHAPTER THIRTEEN

A couple days passed, and Saturday finally arrived. Bree had been feeling jittery ever since Scott's threat. When he went after Denver, she'd been scared he might have a knife or a gun. They were lucky he hadn't. She was relieved when he didn't show up at the Lakeshore Bar again. Denver had met her after work each night and followed her home, just to be safe. Bree hoped that their unity had scared Scott off. If not, the night in jail could have been very convincing.

But this was Saturday; it wasn't easy, but she had gotten the day off. Her parents and Steven were coming, and Bree was too preoccupied getting ready to worry much about Scott. She put on blue jean shorts and a T-shirt to be comfortable while cleaning and getting lunch ready. She had her small window air conditioner and a fan going to keep the apartment from getting too hot. It was going to reach the nineties before the day was over.

Denver had on shorts and a T-shirt himself. It was a little hotter than he liked. He was accustomed to his home that kept cool in the shade from the woods, and the Nighthawk with the breeze from the lake, but as for the businesses in town, it was perfect Fourth of July weather. The beaches would be packed, and Lake Michigan would entertain more boaters than any other day of the year. Denver planned on being one of those boaters, taking Bree's family out on the lake that evening to see the fireworks.

"Can I help you with anything?" he asked as he watched Bree.

"Sure, you can cut these onions and I'll cut the tomatoes. I think I'll wait until they get here to cook the meat and fry the shells. I wanted to make something a little more special, but this apartment is already warm. I didn't want to use the oven."

"I think they'll appreciate that," Denver said as he pulled on the front of his shirt and shook it to get some air.

When one o'clock came, she started to get nervous. "Why aren't they here yet?"

"It's a long drive, and it's the Fourth."

"I know, but they were going to leave early."

"I wouldn't worry," Denver said casually. "They probably got stuck in traffic."

"I guess I should expect that for a big holiday. I'm just anxious to see them. I went down there for Christmas, but I haven't seen them since."

About five minutes later, Bree heard a horn. She ran and opened the door. "It's Steven! Steven's here!" she yelled to Denver and ran down the steps to greet him. Denver followed her at a slow pace to allow her time to greet her brother and say hello.

They gave each other a hug. "Nice jeep," Steven said finally. "It must belong to this Denver I've been hearing about. It can't be yours."

"And why not?"

"If it's yours, I'd like to know what kind of tips you're making and where I can get a job like that."

Bree laughed. She hardly thought Steven would put an apron on and serve tables, especially since he was an engineer like their dad.

By this time, Denver had made his way over to the two of them. Steven was about six feet tall and slim. He had blond hair that was cut short on the back and sides, but thicker on top with bangs. Bree introduced them and they shook hands.

"How was the drive from Grand Rapids?" Denver asked.

"I think we're in for a wild Fourth," Steven answered with a grimace. "People are acting just a little bit weirder than usual."

"Thanks for the warning," Denver said.

They continued their guy talk while Bree stood nearby, watching and listening. She had known they would get along. They both were easygoing and had similar interests.

"Perfect timing," Bree said, as another car pulled into the driveway. Bree and Steven walked over to greet their parents, and Denver followed. Steven definitely took after his father. He was tall and slender and had thinning blond hair. Bree's mother now wore glasses and was of average height. She had short, wavy, dark-blonde hair that was being taken over by gray.

"Mom, Dad," Bree said, "I'd like you to meet Denver. Denver, this is my mom and dad."

"Nice to meet you, Mr. and Mrs. Darby," Denver said as he shook their hands.

"Please," Mr. Darby answered, "call us Tom and Betty. We're not that formal in this family. Besides, I've heard enough about you that I feel like I know you already."

"Come on," Bree said, "I haven't mentioned him *that* much."

"More than you realize," he teased her. "I'm more worried about Denver taking you away from me than Louis." He faked a scowl as he looked over at Denver.

"Don't listen to him," Bree said. "He's always kidding around."

"You guys must be hungry," she added, remembering her job as hostess. "Mom and I will go in and get things ready. It should be done in half an hour."

"That'd be great, 'cause I'm starved," Steven responded.

The men stayed outside while Bree and Betty finished cooking. When the men came in, the taco meat, shells, chopped vegetables, cheese, and sour cream were on the table. Bree and Betty filled glasses for them and they all sat down to eat. For dessert, Bree brought out the traditional Fourth of July cake that she had baked the night before and decorated that morning. It had whipped cream on it, with rows of strawberries for the stripes and blueberry stars to make it look like the American flag.

"That was good," Denver said when they were finished. "I think I ate too much."

"She's a good cook, just like her mom," Tom said proudly.

"I did learn from the best," Bree said. Sometimes she took things for granted, but lately she had been thinking about her parents a lot, realizing just how lucky she was. They never made her feel like an outsider or unwanted. She knew she could always count on them.

After dishes were cleared and they were all sitting in the living room, Tom brought the subject around to what was on all their minds.

"So," he said to Bree. "Tell us all about Louis."

"Oh, he's great," Bree blurted out, without thinking: she sounded more enthused than she'd intended. She tried to hide some of her excitement, but it was not easily accomplished. "He's from Italy and speaks with an accent. I have a couple pictures, if you'd like to see them."

"Of course we would," Betty said.

Bree went into the bedroom and brought out the pictures. "This one is of my birth parents and me. I must have been just under two years old when it was taken."

Betty reached out for it and held it in front of her. When she looked at the picture her face went pale, as if she had just seen a ghost pass in front of her. She took a deep breath and let it out as she put her hand to her chest. "Oh my, oh my," she kept saying. "That little girl is you. I would bet my life on it. You look just like your mother," she said in a squeaky voice. "Tom, you have got to see this," she said, handing the picture to her husband. Bree sat next to her mom and put her arm around her. They were both getting teary-eyed.

"Uh huh," he said, nodding his head. "That's you alright. Did Louis give you this picture?"

"The private detective he hired did," Bree said, quickly moving the conversation along without looking in Denver's direction.

At the mention of Scott, Denver scowled and rolled his eyes.

Tom and Betty were listening so intently to everything Bree was saying that they didn't notice, but Steven did. He silently wondered what it was that was bothering Denver, but said nothing.

"Hey, Denver," Steven asked after a while, "you wouldn't by any chance let me drive that jeep of yours and show me around town, would you?"

"Sounds good to me. Would you like to go right now?"

"That would be great."

The two of them excused themselves and headed outside. Denver tossed him the keys.

"This ride's smooth," Steven said, after they had driven for a while.

"Yah," Denver answered, teasing, "You drive it almost as good as your sister."

"Hey, watch it," he said, laughing. "Speaking of Bree, that's one of the reasons I dragged you out here."

Denver nodded. "It was a good idea to give them some time alone."

"That too, but what I really wanted was to ask you some questions. I noticed that you weren't quite as enthused as Bree was about some of the things she was saying."

Denver hesitated a moment. "Was I that obvious?"

"Just a little, but don't worry. Mom and Dad didn't notice a thing. They've always been a little blind where Bree's concerned."

Denver wondered just how much he should tell Steven. If he got everyone in the family upset, Bree would be furious. He had hard, concrete reasons for not liking Scott, but everything else was just based on a feeling or a hunch. He knew he couldn't tell him about his grandmother's premonitions. He would sound like the village idiot—not the kind of impression you want to give your girlfriend's family the first day you meet them.

Denver decided to take a chance and trust Steven. Even though Bree said they hadn't gotten along well when they were little, he could tell that had changed. He had a feeling Steven only wanted what was best for Bree.

"I do have some suspicions," Denver said. "Can I trust you to keep what I say between us? I know Bree wouldn't want her mom and dad to worry."

Steven nodded, sensing that he wasn't going to like what he was about to hear. "You have my word."

"I suppose," Denver said, "if Louis had to hire a private detective over here from Italy, maybe he had no clue of the kind of guy he was hiring. But his detective, Scott, is lower than a cockroach. He's been coming to the bar and harassing Bree. I've been going in each night and following her home to make sure she gets there safely. A few nights ago, Scott got so out of line that I went over and talked to him. It didn't do any good."

"What did you do?"

"I hauled off and punched him. Gave him a fat lip to remember me by."

"You did?"

"Don't get the wrong impression. I don't make it a habit to hit people or get in fights, but I didn't like the way he was talking to Bree and leering at her. I lost control."

"Wow," Steven said, leaning back against the seat and staring ahead. He had pulled into a parking lot so he could listen carefully to everything Denver said. "Is he still bothering Bree?"

"Not for the last couple days, but that night after I hit him he threatened to make all of us pay."

"This doesn't sound good. I'm glad you were there to help her. Did you tell Louis what the detective he hired was doing?"

"No."

"Why not?"

Denver frowned.

"Don't tell me there's something wrong with Louis, too."

"No, as far as I can tell he's okay."

"As far as you can tell? There's more, isn't there?"

"I don't know," Denver said, shrugging his shoulders in frustration. "I shouldn't say anything, because it's just a feeling I have. It's probably my imagination, but this whole situation just doesn't feel right to me. Maybe I'm being overprotective or something."

"Tell me, and I'll decide for myself."

"Louis is perfect," Denver said, throwing his arms up in despair. "He says all the right things, acts the way you would expect him to act in this situation. He's very proper."

"So, what's the problem?"

"Patrizia, her mother, is the problem. According to Louis, she just flew to the United States and abandoned Bree with strangers. Why would she do that? Because she was jealous of an affair he had? Does she look like the kind of person that would do that?"

"I don't know. I didn't really look at the picture that closely."

"When we get back, take another good, long look at the picture and tell me what you think. I hope you can tell me I'm crazy."

"So do I," Steven answered as he put the jeep in gear. "So do I."

When they got back to Bree's apartment, everyone looked relaxed. They'd had enough time to say whatever needed to be said, and everyone seemed to be accepting the new developments in Bree's life.

Denver was especially glad of Steven's acting abilities. No one had a clue as to the seriousness of the conversation they'd had while they were gone.

"I think I'll have a beer," Steven said, getting out of his chair and heading towards the kitchen. "It's a little warm in here."

"Since when do you need an excuse to have a beer?" Bree teased him.

"If you have a good one, you might as well use it," he answered as he made himself at home, grabbing a can and popping it open. On the kitchen table, he saw the pictures of Bree and her birth parents. He picked up the family picture. He sat down at the table and stared at it. At first, all he saw was a normal, happy family.

But he did as Denver had suggested and looked at it longer. The man in the picture, Louis, held the baby in one arm and had his other arm wrapped around the woman. He had a confident smile on his face—a controlled, smug look. The woman looked small next to him, not so much in size as in timidity. She was smiling, but it was a tired smile. Her eyes had a depth to them that drew you in when you looked closely. What was he seeing? Was it fear, despair, or sorrow? Perhaps all three. All Steven knew was that he agreed with Denver. She did not look like someone who could ruthlessly leave her child just for spite and never look back.

An uneasiness swept through him; when he looked up, his eyes locked with Denver's across the room. Denver knew instantly that they had come to the same conclusions.

That evening, Denver took all of them out on the Nighthawk. They were just coming out of the harbor and entering the waters of Lake Michigan when Betty exclaimed, "Oh, look," pointing to a boat. "There's the United States Coast Guard."

"They always have their boats out on the Fourth," Denver explained. "The Coast Guard Station is back around the bend we just passed."

"That's nice to know," Steven said, "just in case some fireworks go astray. Where do they shoot them from?"

"Off that breakwater over there," Denver answered, pointing to his right. "It's going to be a while before they start, so I thought I'd head north to show you some of the Sleeping Bear shoreline. We can be back in the Frankfort area by the time it gets dark."

"Sounds like a plan," Steven answered.

Denver normally kept the back cleared, except for a cushioned cooler, so there was room for fishing, but he had brought some boat seats aboard for tonight. Steven sat in the chair next to Denver while Bree and her parents sat astern.

They were enjoying the scenery while they talked. Suddenly Betty stood up. "Don't tell me," she said excitedly, "that must be Point Betsie. I've never seen it from the water before."

They all looked towards the shore. It was a long distance away, but you could make out the lighthouse, the row of Lombardy trees, and the lifesaving station. Each person was silent in his or her own thoughts. Point Betsie stirred poignant memories in all of them.

It was Tom who broke the silence. "That's where we found our little girl—a gift from heaven."

Tom wasn't necessarily a religious man. He never went to church and only thought of God occasionally, but when he thought of his wife and two children, he truly felt blessed. Although he never voiced his fears to others, he always worried that whoever abandoned Bree at Point Betsie would someday come back to claim her, but they never did. Now that she was an adult, nobody could force her to go anywhere. Whatever happened now would be her choice. It was a relief to have that burden lifted.

"Yes," Betty added. "We already had the boy we wanted, and had been discussing whether it was time to have another child. And then there you were. The timing and everything seemed too perfect to be true. On that day, I was given a little girl and I didn't even have to go through the diapers-and-bottles stage again—not to mention another pregnancy."

"She came housebroken," Steven said jokingly, as only a big brother could.

"Thanks a lot!" Bree said, laughing.

Betty ignored their comments, still remembering back to that day. She had never really shared with Bree any details of what happened, figuring it was best that way, but Bree was old enough to know everything now.

"I couldn't believe it when I read that note," Betty said. "I thought it had to be some kind of sick joke. Someone would leave a baby by those rocks and busted-up cement? Tom and I ran over there and found out it was true. I looked around and there was no one in sight, so I reached out to pick you up and you started screaming. I didn't know what to do. We couldn't leave you there on the rocks." Betty swallowed hard before continuing. She kept her eyes off Bree and fixed on the shore.

"You were crying for your mama and looking around for her. You had beautiful dark curls and the biggest, most fearful brown eyes I had ever seen. Tears were streaming down your cheeks. It took a lot of coaxing but I was finally able to convince you to let me pick you up. After that, you wouldn't let go. Even the lady from Child Services didn't have the heart to take you from me. Tom and I talked and we decided we wanted to take care of you until your parents were found. They did a background check on us. When it came back alright, they pushed papers through as fast as possible to make us your foster parents until it was decided what to do with you.

"Many couples wanted to adopt you. By the time they needed to make a decision, you were already a part of our family, so we petitioned to adopt you. Since Social Services spoke in our favor and the public was on our side, it was an easy choice. We were granted legal guardianship until enough time had passed that we could legally adopt you."

"Why haven't you wanted to tell me all this before?" Bree asked. "You always looked hurt if I asked any questions. I felt guilty whenever I did, so I quit asking."

"You don't understand what it was like for us," Betty answered, turning to look at Bree. "For a long time, you wouldn't let me out of your sight. You couldn't sleep unless I was lying next to you. The people from Social Services tried to get you to talk to them so they could get clues as to where you came from, but no one had any luck. You cried often and you seldom took your thumb out of your mouth. The rare times you did, the few words you said sounded like nothing more than mumbling. The only thing anyone understood was 'Mama.' You had to learn how to talk all over again. The psychiatrist thought it was the trauma of being abandoned, and no one really knew what else you might've gone through. Now I understand why you wouldn't talk. You were in a strange land surrounded by people that didn't even speak your language. It must've been awful for you. Once you finally started coming around, I wanted to get that part of your life behind you. I never wanted you to look for your birth parents. You suffered so much when you were little that I didn't want to see you hurt again. I worried that maybe your birth parents would reject you and you would feel abandoned all over again. I wish I could say my only motives were to protect you, but I didn't want to lose you either. That was selfish of me. Forgive me for not being more open with you, but I just wanted all of us to have a normal, happy life."

Tears were streaming down Betty's face as she turned away.

"Oh, Mom," Bree said, crying as she stood up to give Betty a hug. "I don't have to forgive you because there's nothing to forgive. You made all the right choices. You did what you thought was best for me, and I love you for it."

"I was so afraid you would find your birth parents when you moved up here and you would forget about us."

"That will never happen, Mom. Never."

They stood there hugging and crying while the guys sniffled and looked the other way. The cry made Bree feel cleansed inside. So many times, she had felt things that could not be explained. Now it all made sense.

When they got back to the Frankfort area, the fireworks were a good recipe to lighten the mood. The sparkling colors reflected soft lights on the water. If you looked over on the breakwater where the fireworks were being shot off, you could see the outline of a man running from one spot to another. A big square shape would light up and shoot the fireworks into the sky.

After the grand finale, they headed back to shore and everyone thanked Denver for taking them out on the Nighthawk. Steven made Denver promise to take him fishing someday soon, so they exchanged phone numbers.

The Darbys spent the night at Bree's apartment and headed home the next day, while Steven went to spend a night or two with an old college friend who lived in the area. He was on vacation and planned to make the most of it.

CHAPTER FOURTEEN

A few weeks had passed since Louis was released from prison and arrived in the United States. The Fourth of July celebration had just ended, and he was feeling quite pleased with himself regarding the progress he was making with Brianna. Having seen her a couple of times already, he knew he was winning her over. He picked up his cell phone to call her.

"Hello, Brianna. This is your papa...Fine, and how are you doing?...That is good. I am calling to see if I could take you out to dinner tonight. I would like you to bring your friend Denver too."

He rocked gently in the rocker and grinned smugly as he waited for her answer.

"I am so glad," he continued. "How does The Fisherman's Knot sound? I was told it has excellent food and a pleasant view of Betsie Lake and the marina...Denver still does not feel comfortable about all this, does he?...No. That is all right. I understand. He is being protective. Maybe he will change his mind after tonight...I do not want to cause trouble. I will meet the two of you at six o'clock. How does that sound?...Good. I will see you tonight...Goodbye."

Louis hung up the phone and kept rocking in the chair. "So, what do you think of my performance?" He waited a moment. "What— no comment? Oh, that is right, you do not have much to say, do you?" he said laughingly, amused with his cleverness. He laughed louder as he watched Patrizia struggling to loosen the ropes tied tightly around her.

"This is a cozy little place you have here, Patrizia. I am impressed. It even has a fireplace." He nodded his approval as he surveyed his surroundings. Walking over to her, he grabbed a corner of the duct tape sealing her mouth and harshly yanked it off. Patrizia cried out from the pain.

"What a shame," Louis said, pretending to be sympathetic. "Your skin looks sore and your lips are swelling up. We cannot have that. You may get to see Brianna again soon. We want you to look your best for that special reunion, now don't we?"

"Louis. Please leave Brianna out of this. I will do whatever you want."

Louis laughed, returning to his chair. "Of course you will do whatever I want. You are hardly in a position to bargain." He drank some of his scotch as he resumed rocking. He was enjoying watching Patrizia squirm.

"For fifteen years I sat in prison, with nothing to think about except what I would do when I got out. While I was locked up, you were enjoying your freedom. Because of you, I have wasted fifteen years of my life and lost some of my status in the organization. I had to beg an old favor to get over here at all. But, such indignity was worth it, so long as I have my vengeance."

"That was not my fault, Louis. You pulled the trigger yourself. You went to jail because you killed an unarmed man in cold blood," Patrizia said, defending herself.

"It never would have happened if you had not left me. Can you imagine the embarrassment I suffered? How can a man who cannot keep his wife under control be respected? I lost a lot of esteem and honor in the eyes of my superiors. You took me by surprise when you showed up in Italy. I let my emotions get in the way and lost control, but not this time. If there is anything I learned in prison, it is how to be patient. Do you remember what I said I would do if you ever left me?"

Patrizia shook her head 'no,' not wanting to remember, but it was in her memory as if he'd said the words yesterday. He would make her and Brianna pay. Closing her eyes, the blood rushed to her head and she broke out in a sweat. She had hoped her suffering would be enough to quench his thirst for revenge, that he'd forget what he'd said so long ago. "No, Louis," she whispered, shaking her head more. "Please, do not hurt her."

"Hurt her? Patrizia, I'm amazed at how little you think of me. I will confess, at first I was going to make you watch her slowly die and then do the same to you, but Scott, my associate, has made me see my error. Perhaps, I was a little hasty. I have changed my mind and decided to let her live. Brianna is quite stunning, as you will see. She has your eyes. It would be a shame to waste such a treasure. Scott has assured me there are those who would pay top dollar for a young lady like her. And you know I could never pass up a lucrative deal."

"Louis! No! Please, please! Don't do this! I'll do anything!" Patrizia begged, tears streaming down her cheeks.

"I have decided to spare her life. I thought you might at least be grateful for that."

Louis twirled the ice around in his glass and began to laugh as Patrizia sobbed. The more she pleaded, the more sinister his laugh became.

"Oh, Patrizia," he said, wiping the tears of laughter from his eyes. "I had forgotten how entertaining you could be." He thought for a moment. "I should use something besides this duct tape when I leave. We want to take care of that delicate skin of yours, but for now I must get ready. I have an important date tonight."

Patrizia sat helplessly in the chair. There was nothing she could do but hope and pray that God would get her and Brianna through this alive.

Denver drove over to Bree's apartment. When she let him in, he let out a whistle and stared at her. "Wow," was all he could say. He had never seen her dressed up before.

Bree laughed. "I take it you like it?" she asked, slowly turning around.

She had on a cotton knee-length dress that clung to her curves. It was a soft peach color, and she had on cream high-heel shoes and held a matching purse. She had taken extra pains to do her makeup and hair just right. Her hair tumbled down to her shoulders in soft, wavy curls.

He walked over to her and put his hands on her waist. "I love it," he said, pulling her close to him and kissing her like he had never kissed her before.

"Now it is my turn to say 'Wow,'" Bree responded breathlessly, as she felt every nerve-ending awakening.

"I wish I didn't have to share you with anyone. I would love it if I could have you to myself tonight," he whispered in her ear.

"I do, too, but Louis will be waiting for us. We have to be going."

"I know," Denver responded, regretfully stepping back to let her go. "You just look so unbelievably gorgeous tonight."

Bree stepped closer to him. "Maybe after dinner we can finish what we started," she said seductively.

He smiled and gave her a quick kiss, but said nothing. Bree was surprised at his casual response, but guessed it was because he knew they had to be leaving for dinner. She touched up her lipgloss again and they left for the restaurant.

When Denver and Bree arrived at The Fisherman's Knot, Louis was already there. He was looking at the water and the boats in the harbor. The south wall was one big window, which allowed for a pleasant view and lightened up the room, giving it a cheery atmosphere.

When Louis saw Denver and Bree approach the table, he stood up. "Brianna, it is so good to see you," he said, giving her a hug.

"It is good to see you too. Thank you for inviting us."

"It is my pleasure." He extended his hand to Denver. "I am glad that you could make it. I can see that Brianna is fond of you, so I hope that we can be friends."

"I hope so too," Denver answered with a smile. He shook Louis's hand. "Bree has been excited about getting to know you."

"Not half as excited as I have been, I assure you," he said. He pulled out Bree's chair and pushed it in for her as she sat down.

"Thank you," Bree said and smiled brightly at him.

The waitress took their orders for drinks and left them menus to look over.

"Let me see," Louis said, glancing at the menu. "Being here, seeing the boats and the harbor, has reminded me of home. We have the best fish there. How does the fish compare here, Denver? What do you recommend?"

"There are many options. They have salmon, if you like that. There's also perch and trout, but what I like most is the smoked whitefish. There's nothing better."

"Yes, I have heard nothing but raves about the whitefish. I think I will be ordering that."

"Excellent choice," Denver said, closing his menu, "I think I'll have the same."

"I would not mind getting some fishing in before I return home," Louis said. "Maybe I will sign up for one of the charter trips in the area."

"That's not a bad idea. There are several good charter fishing companies to choose from, but if you'd like, I could take you for a trip on the Nighthawk."

"You would do that?"

"Sure. Why not?"

"I just might take you up on your most generous offer. Where do you go?"

"It depends on the time of year and what I'm fishing for, but there's a hole about six miles off Point Betsie. I go there often."

"I see. Just north of there are some islands and I saw a lighthouse on the southeast corner. Are these waters rough?"

"They can be. The lighthouse marks the beginning of the Manitou Passage. In the past, many boats and ships would stop at the east bay of South Manitou Island when they knew a storm was coming in. It's a good place to take refuge and wait out bad weather. You do have to be careful of the shoals around the islands and along the shoreline, though. If you don't know where they are you could easily hit one. In storms, it's easy to get stranded."

"Sounds like you know your business," Louis said approvingly.

"You've got to. People have gotten into trouble because of inexperience and stupid mistakes."

"I can imagine that is true."

The waitress came back to take their order. Denver and Louis ordered the whitefish and Bree ordered soup and a salad.

"Is that all you are ordering?" Louis asked. "Dinner is on me. Order whatever you wish."

"The soup and salad will be plenty," Bree assured him. "While you two were talking, I've been munching on these rolls. They're delicious."

"Ah," Louis nodded. "You are a light eater. That is how you keep that slim figure of yours. You look beautiful tonight."

"She certainly does," Denver agreed enthusiastically.

"Now be careful," Louis kidded. "That is my little girl you are talking about."

Bree laughed. "Will you two stop it? You're embarrassing me."

"What?" Louis asked, lifting his arms in a gesture of despair. "Is not a father allowed to brag about his girl?"

"If you insist," Bree conceded, "please continue."

Louis and Denver laughed. They decided mutually that it would be best not to overdo the compliments for a while.

"Denver," Louis said, changing the subject, "Brianna tells me that you work with your relatives and they have a commercial fishing business. If you do not mind, I would love to hear about it."

"Sure, I don't mind at all. Most people want to know what we catch, and that's whitefish and lake trout. We use nets and pack the fish in ice to keep them fresh. Is there anything in particular that you are interested in? There are many things I could talk about."

"Yes, I imagine that is true." He thought a second before continuing. "Every industry has its rewards and challenges. What is your greatest challenge?"

"Everyone has their own opinion on what that is, because there are many challenges. Personally, the thing that worries me the most is invasive species. It can be a huge problem for everyone."

"Ahh, yes. Nature has a delicate balance that needs to be maintained. What is causing the most problems?"

"In the past it's been things like zebra mussels and round gobies, and the list goes on; but what's worrying me now is the Asian carp that have made their way up the Mississippi River and across the Illinois River. If they make it into Lake Michigan, the damage could be irreversible. Electric barriers stop them, but if they fail..." Denver stopped and shook his head. "The ecosystem will be negatively affected. Asian carp have voracious appetites and will devour the food the native fish live on. They have a rapid reproduction rate and are large in size."

"That does not sound good at all."

"No. The impact will be devastating. The silver carp are known for jumping up to ten feet out of the water when they hear boat and jet-ski motors, causing physical harm to people and property. Normally, the silver carp are around twenty pounds and the bighead carp about forty pounds, but they've been known to reach 110 pounds and get as long as sixty inches."

"Amazing. I can see where this would be a problem."

"Yes, it's definitely a problem. What's sad is, if they would've left nature alone we wouldn't even be worrying about this. Over one hundred years ago, they reversed the flow of the Chicago River. Some people are talking about reversing it again."

"They reversed the flow of the river?" Louis said, slapping the table, shaking his head and laughing in disbelief. "The audacity! Next they will want to move the ocean!"

"I wouldn't be surprised."

"It is amazing that something like that is even possible. Did they not think there might be dire consequences?"

"At the time, Lake Michigan was severely polluted around the Chicago area. They had to do something because Chicago residents got their drinking water from Lake Michigan and people were getting seriously ill. Reversing the river was the answer to that problem for Chicago, but their neighbors to the west of them weren't happy. The polluted waters were flowing into the Illinois and Mississippi rivers."

Louis shook his head in dismay. "That is not good. There never seems to be a perfect answer."

"No, there isn't. It all began with the pollution of the Great Lakes. We need to be wiser about how we treat our environment. It set off a chain of events. Once one problem is resolved, we find we're facing another."

"That is the way it seems to go."

"Almost always. I don't mean to pick on Chicago—all the big cities and all of us as individuals have been guilty of harming the environment—but at this moment I'm worried about the Asian carp."

They continued their conversation while eating, until the waitress came to give them their bill. The topic had been somber, but Bree was glad to see the two of them talking and enjoying each other's company. She was relieved Denver was coming around and accepting Louis.

"As you can see," Bree said to Louis, "Denver is passionate about the environment and his work."

Louis nodded approvingly. "That is good. If a man does not have passion, he has nothing." He wiped his hands on his napkin. "Now I have something I would like to show you," he said, dramatically reaching for a document sitting on the empty chair. He handed Bree and Denver each a copy. "I believe, Denver and Brianna, that you have been wanting to see this. I received it yesterday and had copies made."

They both looked over the official-looking document that was written in Italian. Neither one could read the words on it, but Bree immediately spotted her name: Brianna. "This is my birth certificate," she said out loud. She gave Louis a hug. "Thank you so much for getting this for me."

"I did not mind doing it. Any time you need anything, just ask and I will see what I can do." He read the document to Bree, pointing out his name, Louis Cipriano, and her mother's name, Patrizia Cipriano. He also showed her the birth date, September fifth.

"September fifth." Tears came to her eyes. "I've just been using the date they found me as my birth date, because I never knew what it was. I don't know what to say. It's like all the missing pieces in my life are finally coming together."

Louis gave her arm a pat. "I feel the same."

Bree nodded and smiled faintly, looking down at her lap. "You said before that you were still looking for Patrizia and you had leads."

"Yes. The search continues...I have several private detectives on the case back in Europe."

"If you want to find her for your own reasons, that's fine," said Bree, "but you don't have to look for her for my benefit. If she wanted to see me it would be one thing, but I'm not interested in meeting someone that wants nothing to do with me."

"I understand why you would feel this way. I do want to find her and talk to her. When I find her, if she is interested in seeing you, I will make arrangements. Otherwise, we will leave things as they are. Does that sound acceptable to you?"

"It sounds fine."

They talked some more, lingering over dinner before rising up to leave. Louis gave Brianna a hug, then shook Denver's hand, saying he would soon take him up on his fishing trip offer.

On the way back to her apartment, Bree sat quietly, deep in thought. The night had gone better than she expected; getting a copy of her birth certificate was the best dessert she could've asked for.

Once inside, Denver sat down on the couch and watched Bree as she went over to the stereo and put on some music. She walked over to him, swaying to the beat, and then sat down and snuggled up next to him.

He was amazed at the feelings and emotions that stirred inside him. They both were silent for a while as they listened to the music.

"What are you thinking?" Denver asked as he gently stroked her arm. "I didn't even think about it at the time, but I'm now realizing that Louis and I dominated the conversation most of the night. That was rude of us not to include you more."

"Oh, that didn't bother me," she said, laughing. "I enjoyed listening to both of you."

"You're quieter than usual. What are you thinking about?"

"I don't know, really. I have so many thoughts running through my mind that it's hard to sort them all out."

"Start with the first thing that pops into your head."

"I guess that would be my birth parents, Louis and Patrizia. How can two people, who are supposedly so in love when they get married, end up hurting each other so terribly? It happens all the time. It seems like everyone ends up getting divorced and hating each other. It's kind of scary."

"That's true. Divorces are common, but there are still many who remain together and stay in love."

"You're right. My adoptive parents are a good example of that."

"Finding the right person is the key. If you do that, the rest should be easy."

Bree smiled as she looked deep into his eyes. He was everything she ever wanted in a man. They seemed to connect on every level. Bree snuggled in closer, gently kissing and caressing him.

Denver let out a low moan and held her close to him. "Bree, there is nothing I want more than to be with you tonight, but I can't stay."

"Why?" she asked, a little surprised.

"Grandmother had another bad spell last night."

"Oh, no! Is she okay?"

"We took her to the hospital. She wasn't in any shape to argue this time. They seem to think it was a mini-stroke, but it doesn't look like any serious damage was done. They're still running tests to be sure, but they think she'll be able to come home tomorrow. They'll put her on medication. What she needs now is to rest and stop worrying. Too much stress could cause another stroke, and we may not be so lucky next time."

"What upset her?"

Denver hesitated to answer. "She had another vision. I've never seen her that frantic before. She's convinced that danger is very near to you now, closer than before."

"Why didn't you tell me all of this earlier? We didn't have to go out tonight."

"You were looking forward to it. I didn't see any reason to disappoint you." He didn't bother to tell her that he was afraid she would go without him if he didn't come.

Bree sat back on the couch, deep in thought. She curled her knees up to her chest and wrapped her arms around them. "Denver, I have something to tell you that I should have told you sooner."

"What is it?"

"I've run into Scott a couple times this week. He never approached me, but the way he smiled at me and the fact that our paths seem to keep crossing each other makes me think he's following me. And, I'm not sure, but I could've sworn I saw a camera in his hand."

"What? That's not something to keep to yourself."

"I was afraid you would overreact. I can take care of myself," Bree answered, but she didn't sound convincing this time.

"Bree, you're not invincible. You've got to be careful and let me know everything that's going on."

"I will. He does give me the creeps," she said, and quickly changed the subject. "Is it all right if I come up to the hospital and see Grandmother?"

"Probably not tonight. Seeing you might upset her more. I'll see how she's doing, and most likely, you should be able to see her tomorrow. She's a tough lady."

"She sure is. I guess I'll see you tomorrow, after work. I have the early shift."

"I'll try to get off work early, but it'll depend on the fishing. I'll give you a call when I'm done." He gave her a kiss and they said goodbye. On his way back up to the hospital, he saw Charlie's car at the Lakeshore Bar, so he pulled in. He went over to the bar and greeted Charlie.

"Hey, Denver. I'm glad you stopped in. I was just thinking about you. Let's sit at that back table and talk. I've been meaning to tell you what we learned about Scott Proctor."

Denver nodded and followed him. He ordered a beer for Charlie.

"When they brought Scott in the other night, they ran a check on him," Charlie said, getting right to the point. "I'm afraid I don't have good news to report—he's certainly no choir boy. He's been convicted of assault and battery, and he also had a rape charge filed against him, but the victim suddenly withdrew the charges and changed her story. How's that for convenience?"

"Damn!" Denver said, running his hand through his hair. "I knew he was trouble."

"That's putting it mildly," added Charlie. "Next time I see him, I'll have a talk with our friend."

"Thanks. It certainly couldn't hurt. Have you heard anything about Louis yet?"

"No," Charlie answered. "That might take some time. Checking records from another country involves more red tape, but I'll let you know as soon as I hear something."

"That would be great. Louis gave us this tonight," he said, handing Charlie the copied birth certificate. "It looks like the real thing, and Louis seems sincere, but I would still like to have everything checked out. Maybe I've been wrong about him—I don't know. He does seem like a nice guy, but I'll feel better having some evidence."

"It doesn't hurt to be careful. I'll check again to see if they have anything back on Louis, and I'll check out the birth certificate too."

Denver nodded and stood up to leave. "I'm going to call Bree to warn her about Scott. Then I've got to get going, but I want you to know how much I appreciate all your help."

"There's no need to thank me. I don't want to see Bree hurt any more than you do."

Denver put some money down on the table for the beer and told Charlie goodbye. He then made a call to Bree and called Steven to let him know what he'd just found out. He had a lot on his mind as he headed up to the hospital. If anything happened to Bree or Grandmother, he didn't know what he'd do.

CHAPTER FIFTEEN

Bree hung up after talking to Denver, and then called Louis. Maybe he could get Scott to leave her alone.

"I am so sorry, Brianna," Louis said. "I did not even know he was still around. I thought after I paid him he would go back to New York. I knew nothing about his record. I was told he was the best at finding missing people. He came highly recommended."

"That's okay. I know you didn't know, but he makes me feel uncomfortable."

"He is probably still at the same hotel room. I will give him a call. I do not appreciate anyone harassing my little girl. Do not worry. I will take care of everything."

After Louis hung up, he sat silently thinking about what he would do next. If they knew about Scott, it was possible they were checking on him also. He knew Denver did not trust him completely. It would only be a matter of time before they learned about his time in prison. He would have to change his plans and move into action immediately. Perhaps his client would be willing to move up the date of their merchandise exchange. Patrizia would know what it was to suffer, and he was not going to go back to prison. Those were the two things he was sure of.

The next day at work was a good one for Bree. They were in the thick of the tourist season and she made quite a bit in tips that morning. Dog-tired and glad that her shift had ended, she hurried to her car, anxious to see how Grandmother was doing.

Stepping outside, Bree noticed the high humidity. The wind was gusting considerably stronger than it had been that morning.

She tossed her purse onto the passenger seat and hopped into her Camaro.

A hand from behind covered her mouth, and a hard object was thrust into her side. "Don't scream and don't make a move," a voice said.

She recognized it. Scott. Panicking, she bit his hand and reached for the handle on the door. He grabbed a handful of her hair and yanked her head back. This time he brought the gun he was holding up to her neck. She could feel the cold steel. "Don't make me use this, Brianna. It would be such a waste. Cooperate—no one gets hurt. Don't cooperate, and whatever happens will be on you."

"Me? I'm not the one with the gun."

"Don't make this difficult. All I want is for you to meet someone."

"Who? You have a strange way of introducing people. Do you think I'm going to believe that's all you want? I know all about you."

"Oh yes, your friend checked everything out, didn't he? He's starting to annoy me, and so are you. It wasn't very polite of you to turn down my hospitality. Aren't you supposed to make the patrons feel welcome?"

Bree shivered. "I was nicer to you than you deserved. What do you want from me?"

Scott laughed, slid his hand onto her shoulder, and whispered in her ear. "Oh, I could think of a few things. Before the business transaction is completed, if you're a good girl, we just might be able to have some fun."

A chill ran through her. "I don't understand what business you're talking about."

"I'm taking you to meet someone. We'll go to the marina and get on a boat that's waiting for us. Cause a scene, and others will get hurt. Your choice. I'm going to get in the front seat now. Don't try anything stupid."

Bree did as she was told and drove. Her mind raced. No way would she let that creep touch her. She had to think of something.

"I can see wheels turning in your head, Miss Brianna. Don't even think of doing anything stupid. When we get to the marina, act naturally and say we're going fishing if anyone asks. Got it?"

"Got it," Bree said through clenched teeth.

When they pulled into the parking lot, she saw the docked boats and instantly thought about Denver. If he was there, he would try to help her and possibly get hurt in the process. She didn't have a choice but to go along with everything for now.

Getting out of the car, Scott took hold of Bree's arm. "Now, is that any way to look when you're with an old friend? Smile, we're buddies, remember?"

Bree glared at him, but tried to act casual as they approached the boats. Frank, who was a licensed captain and owner of a charter fishing company, was taking care of his equipment as they passed.

"Hey, Bree, what's up?" he asked. "You're not goin' out now, are ya? A storm's comin' in tonight and the big pond will be roilin'."

Bree could feel the pressure of Scott's grip tighten, but he was relaxed and grinning.

"We're just going on a short fishing trip. We'll be back in before long," she said. A thought came to her and she added, "Tell Denver I'm going to try fishing the right way—using his grandmother's tips."

"You don't have much time. Storms don't wait for no one."

Scott kept Bree moving and motioned for her to board a rental boat called the Kinsley. It was a 2008 Sea Ray 290 Sundancer.

"Sit down," he said as he started the boat. She sat and looked back at the shore slipping away. An overwhelming sense of hopelessness filled her. Maybe she should've run for it at the marina and screamed for help. She wasn't sure, but it was too late now.

"Enjoying the ride, Brianna?"

"Hardly," Bree answered, taking a good, long look at Scott. He handled the boat with ease, obviously experienced. When she looked to the northwest and saw the cumulus clouds forming, she began to wonder if Scott's skills might be put to the test. Right now, they looked white and harmless as cotton, but that could quickly change.

"Did you do a lot of boating in New York? Lake Michigan can get rough in storms. We shouldn't be out here," Bree said, forcing herself to be as friendly to him as she could stomach. It didn't sit well with her, but she was at Scott's mercy for the moment. Sooner or later, Denver would wonder where she was. Believing he would figure it out was her only hope.

"I've piloted boats on the Atlantic. Your Great Lakes should be a breeze."

Bree tried to keep silent. His cocky attitude was grating. Finally, she had to say something. "The bones of many expert seamen lie at the bottom of this lake you call a 'breeze.' What makes you think you're better than them, or more powerful than a storm?"

Scott laughed. "You won't find my bones down there. The storm's not supposed to hit for a while; we should have just enough time to get north of it before it passes through. Wouldn't want to miss our business rendezvous." He flashed her a leering grin.

"Storms aren't predictable. You don't know for certain."

He turned and glared at her. "I know what I'm doing. I can handle whatever comes up."

Bree glared back but said nothing.

Scott kept a steady pace until the shore was a long way off, then slowed the boat. "It's show time, Brianna."

"What does that mean?" A deep quiver traveled up her spine, lifting the hair at the nape of her neck.

"There's someone below deck waiting to meet you. Go on," he said, nodding to the steps leading down.

Bree took a step backward and looked over the edge. Waves were slapping the side of the boat.

"You're not that crazy, are you? You wouldn't get far."

Bree said nothing, knowing he was right.

"You can go down on your own, or I can help you. Your choice."

"I'll go alone," she said.

Scott accelerated as Bree slowly made her way down. She extended her arms to the side walls to steady herself. She felt like she was descending into a tomb.

Reaching the bottom, she stopped and stared in disbelief at a woman who was gagged and tied to a chair. Tears were streaming down the woman's cheeks and her eyes were wild with fear. She struggled against the ropes, making a muffled sound. She kept jerking her head to the right and looking in that direction, trying to tell Bree something.

Bree took a few steps forward, wanting to help the woman.

"Brianna, it is so nice to see you," came a voice from behind her. Bree turned around.

"Louis?" she said, stunned. "What's going on? What are you doing here?"

"I thought it might be fun to have a little family reunion. I have been wanting the three of us to get together for a long time. Brianna, this is Patrizia."

"This is my mom?" Bree asked, turning to look at the woman she had spent a lifetime wondering about. "I don't understand why you have her tied up like that. I told you I didn't want to meet her."

"Yes, you did, but I do not agree. I felt that a family get-together was of utmost importance. Patrizia, as you see, was not accommodating. She is good at disappearing and I could not take a chance of that happening again."

"Well, she can't get far out here on the boat. I'm going to untie her." Bree made a motion to head in that direction.

"Stop."

There was a coldness in his tone that made her freeze. Bree turned and looked at him. "You can't leave her tied up like that!"

"Oh, but I can, and I will."

He chuckled as he went over and took the cloth gag, none too gently, off of Patrizia. The two women stared at each other.

Patrizia tried to speak. Her mouth was sore and as dry as ashes. "I am so sorry," Patrizia finally said. "I never wanted this to happen." Tears rolled down her cheeks as she angrily jerked at the ropes.

"I don't understand what's going on," Bree said, stepping towards Louis.

"He is not your father," Patrizia cut in. "He is using you to hurt me. He wants revenge."

"Is that true?" she asked Louis.

Louis chuckled, ignoring Bree. "My, my, Patrizia. You are scaring the poor girl. Is that how you want to act at your reunion with your daughter?"

"Brianna, his plan is to sell you to human traffickers and kill me."

"What? That can't be true! Louis, that isn't true, is it?"

"Brianna, dear. This is not something I wanted. Your mother took you when you were young and left me. Substantial damage was done to my credibility in the organization. This is all because of Patrizia. I had to figure out a way to restore my reputation. Scott had the ingenious plan to turn this into a profit-making adventure as well. Killing you would be such a waste. The pictures Scott got for me of you created quite an interest. The bidding war is bringing me a satisfying profit. Plus, my reputation will, once again, be intact. It will be known everywhere not to mess with Louis Cipriano. This can only help my position with my colleagues. So, you see, Patrizia left me with few options."

"Are you serious? This can't be happening!" Bree said, stepping backward and shaking her head. "This is crazy. I believed every word you said!" She glared at Louis, hoping to see something... remorse, some compassion, anything.

There was nothing. His cold and emotionless steel-blue eyes returned her glare. Bree knew at that moment she had to keep her thoughts clear. This man, who she thought she was starting to know so well, was out to destroy them. Bree looked at Patrizia. So often she had imagined what it would be like to meet her mother. Not in the wildest scenarios she concocted was their meeting anything like this. None of the rehearsed lines fit.

Patrizia looked away, unable to handle the anguish she saw in Bree's eyes.

A gentle but ever-increasing rocking motion had begun as soon as Bree descended into the cabin. Now, without warning, the boat pitched violently to one side. There was a sudden, howling gust of wind. Bree and Patrizia screamed, sure they were going over, but the boat rolled back into its upward position.

"Damn!" Louis yelled, and went up the steps. "I thought you said this would be easy!"

The clouds had grown considerably darker and were piling upward in an angry tower. The two men yelled at each other above the blasting wind. What had been a gentle rocking of the boat became intense. Bree grabbed hold of the table to steady herself.

"I'm going to untie you," Bree said.

"No! You have not seen Louis's temper, and you do not want to."

Bree backed off. "We'll get out of this. Denver will be looking for me. We're going to make it."

Patrizia tried to give a reassuring smile, but she knew Louis too well to be that confident.

CHAPTER SIXTEEN

The commercial fishing boat soon came in and docked to let Denver off. Because Denver had to get up to the hospital, he left right away. In a hurry, he rushed up the dock.

Frank saw him. "You're in early too. Didn't like the looks of what's brewin', did ya?"

"Heck, no. It doesn't look pretty, and the barometer's been dropping steadily."

"I guess it's a good day to quit early anyways. The fish just weren't bitin'. If your grandmother knows some fishin' secrets, maybe you should let me in on 'em. I could've used some help today."

"What are you talking about? Grandmother's never fished a day in her life. What would she know about it?"

Frank looked baffled. "Bree said she was goin' fishin' and she was gonna try out your grandmother's secrets."

"Bree knows my grandmother doesn't fish. When did you talk to her? Was she here?"

Frank shuffled uncomfortably. "She left about an hour ago, with some guy on the Kinsley. She said they'd only be gone for a little while, but she hasn't come back yet."

"What did he look like?"

"In his twenties. Blond hair. That's all I remember."

"Did she say anything else—anything at all?"

"No. What's goin' on?"

"I think Bree's been kidnapped."

"Holy hell! Are you serious?"

"Yes. I'm getting the Nighthawk ready to go look for her." Before Frank could ask more questions, Denver was on his cell phone.

"Charlie, this is Denver. Scott has Bree. He took her out on the Kinsley."

"Damn! That's not good. When did he take her?"

"Maybe half an hour ago. I'm not sure."

Charlie hesitated for a second. "I have some news you're not going to like."

"What is it?" Denver asked, pacing back and forth.

"I've got the results from that check I did on Louis. The birth certificate was authentic. Louis is listed as Bree's father, but he has a record."

"Not as bad as Scott's, I hope."

"No. It's worse."

"Worse than assault and battery or rape?" Denver asked, not believing what he was hearing.

"Try murder."

Denver's mind was spinning. Bree was out there with Scott, and possibly Louis was with them too.

"Denver! You still there?"

"Yes. I'm going after her."

"I'm calling the Coast Guard. They'll handle it."

"Good. Do that, but I'm still going. I can't wait here not knowing if..."

"Well, wait 'til I get there. Scott's rap sheet is longer than a spool of fishing line. I'm only a few minutes away."

"Hurry." He hung up the phone. The wind whipped at him, the sky growing angrier by the minute. It was something he could relate to.

"I'm comin' with you," Frank said.

"It'll be dangerous."

"I figured that."

"Not just the storm. The man with Bree has a record and a gun. Charlie's on his way here."

"Don't matter. I owe you, and I'm not leavin' this boat."

"Let's get this vessel prepared for the worst, then."

Denver did a quick, last-minute check. Plenty of gas. Equipment working. Everything latched down or put away. Enough life jackets on board for passengers and extras.

He put on his wet suit. As he came back up he could hear Charlie's car squealing into the parking lot, but he didn't notice the man walking towards him on the dock.

"Hey, Denver, you're not going out there in this, are you?" Steven asked.

Denver turned around, surprised to see him. He didn't know what to say.

"After you called last night, I thought I'd come back to talk to Bree, but she's not at her apartment or work, and she hasn't answered my calls. Do you know where she is?"

Steven followed Denver's gaze and saw Charlie running towards them.

Steven turned to Denver and paled. "What's going on? Where's Bree?"

"We think Scott has Bree. We're going to look for her."

"You've got to be kidding. Tell me you're not serious!" Steven didn't wait for an answer. "I'm coming with you," he said and stepped aboard. With Charlie right behind him, they quickly pushed off.

CHAPTER SEVENTEEN

On the Kinsley, Scott and Louis yelled at each other over the sound of the howling wind. Scott held on, his knuckles white and cold.

"We almost capsized!" Louis said. "You told me you were the best! What is your problem?"

"I've never seen anything like this! The waves I've been on were bigger, but not as steep. We should change course and head for shelter in East Bay."

"Denver said there are too many shoals. Keep heading west of South Manitou."

"Louis, I've researched these waters. The shoals are near shore. I just have to stay in the middle. Ships have taken shelter off South Manitou in East Bay for years. It's our best chance. The meeting can be rescheduled."

Louis hesitated. "I hired you for your skills and experience. I will let you do as you say, but if you are wrong..." He moved closer, inches from Scott's face. "If you are wrong, you will spend the rest of your short, miserable life looking over your shoulder."

Shivering, Scott nodded, taking the waves at an angle. With each wave, water washed over the deck and the boat rocked.

Louis went back down into the cabin, and water rushed in with him. The bilge pumps were working overtime.

Scott waited for a smaller set of waves. While in the trough, he sharply turned the boat around, with careful attention to speed.

Too much throttle would throw them over the top of the wave. Too little, and they would be swamped from behind. Determined to reach East Bay, he focused on riding the waves. Once the storm subsided, they could continue with Louis's plan.

Seeing the light from South Manitou Lighthouse, Scott kept distance from the shore, but not enough. He was too close. A big wave caught the boat, hurling the vessel over the crest; it plummeted straight down onto a shoal. The hull scraped along the rock-embedded sand, swinging the boat sideways. Scott slammed into the wheel, and below deck Louis and Bree were thrown across the cabin against the wall as loose items pelted them. Bree gasped as the wind was knocked out of her.

Charging up the steps, Louis grabbed the front of Scott's shirt, shoving him against the wheel. "What the hell was that? This is exactly what I did not want to happen!"

"Easy. Easy," Scott said, trying to calm Louis down. "There wasn't supposed to be a shoal here. I studied the charts, but with currents this strong, sands can shift."

"Excuses! You are lucky I need your help right now. If I did not, I would throw you overboard!" he said, giving Scott a shove.

"There's a life raft," Scott said. "I'll get it inflated. This boat has major damage from the shoal and the beating it's taking from the waves isn't helping any. Our only chance is to take the life boat and get to shore."

"I will go down to get what we need," Louis said, descending the steps and walking thigh-deep in water.

Seeing Louis, Patrizia pleaded with him. "You can't leave us here, Louis! We'll drown!"

"Oh dear," Louis answered, feigning sympathy. "I never thought of that. What shall we do?" He then became serious. "This is not quite the ending I had planned. I will not get to enjoy your tearful goodbyes as you watch Brianna go off with her new owners." He grabbed what he needed and the extra life preservers, then headed up the stairs.

"Louis!" Patrizia said. "At least let Brianna go. She is innocent!"

"Innocent is not the name I would give to a barmaid, but what did I expect from a daughter of yours? It has been nice seeing you again, Patrizia, and it has been a pleasure meeting you, Brianna." He turned and continued up the steps and began to help with the life raft.

In a few minutes, Scott came down, wading through the water to grab a few items.

"Get something to smash the radio with," Louis hollered down to Scott. "We must leave them no communication abilities!"

"Will do," Scott answered, saluting. He sloshed through the water over to the cabinets and tugged on the bottom door, which was held shut by the water. After a couple good tugs, he had it open. He pulled out the water-filled tool box and heaved it up onto the counter while water poured out of it.

Rifling through it, he found a wrench. Smiling, he palmed it in his hand. "This will do nicely."

"Scott, please," Bree said. "Help us. Don't let us drown. Get us out of this mess!"

He turned to look at her. "Oh," he said, "*Now* you need Scotty. You wanted nothing to do with me before." He slowly took a couple sloshing steps toward her, swinging the wrench loosely at his side. "I just realized that there's no reason to be careful with the merchandise anymore."

Bree backed up a few steps until bumping against a wall, unable to move any further.

"No! Nooo!" Patrizia screamed. She was frantically jerking so hard on the ropes that her skin began to bleed. She wailed hysterically, calling down curses on Scott.

Paralyzing fear overtook Bree. Unable to scream or react, she stared at Scott, shaking uncontrollably.

Turned on by the fear in Bree's eyes coupled with the frantic screams of Patrizia, Scott stepped up close to Bree. Taking the wrench, he brought it up and began rubbing it against her cheek; his face was inches from hers, grinning wickedly.

Bree stood helpless, her body trembling.

Scott lowered the wrench, trailing it down the length of her left arm. Raising his other hand behind Bree's head, he grabbed a fistful of her hair, yanking her face towards him. He pressed his body roughly against hers and covered her mouth with his and kissed her. Hard.

Unable to get her breath, Bree panicked and fought back with all her strength, but Scott overpowered her.

When he released her, he took a step back, his glare daring her to say something.

Bree yelled at him. "You bastard!"

Whack! Scott slapped her. Hard. The force sent Bree reeling. Shocked, she brought her hand up to her cheek and began to sob uncontrollably.

"Yah," Scott said, nodding and grinning satisfactorily. "If I had more time, I could've taught you some manners."

He went up the steps, hesitating for a second to look back, then continued up to join Louis in the life raft.

Louis looked at him and grinned his approval. "With the amateur mistakes you have made, I was beginning to think you were worthless," he yelled. "But, I have never been able to get Patrizia to scream like that. You are not a total screw-up after all."

"Gee, thanks," Scott yelled back, his hold tightening on the wrench. He walked over to the captain's chair and began to whale on the radio, smashing it to pieces. He then left the boat and joined Louis in the life raft. They pushed off to head for the island, neither sparing a backwards glance at the storm-wracked Kinsley.

Patrizia remained silent, giving Bree time to cry and absorb everything that was happening. When she was sure they were gone, she spoke up.

"Brianna, are you all right?"

Bree nodded, her sobs slowing down to a soft cry and hiccups.

"They are gone now. We do not have much time."

Bree slowly looked over at Patrizia and was alarmed at what she saw. The water was now up to Patrizia's chest. The water currents were shifting the boat and causing it to settle further into the water. Patrizia was white as chalk and looked nauseous.

Bree's determination returned as she wiped the tears from her face. "A knife. I need a knife. Have you seen one?"

"The drawer to the right of the sink."

Wading over to the cupboard, Bree opened the drawer and grabbed a knife. Quickly she went over to Patrizia and cut through the rope binding her wrists. Next, she took a deep breath and dove under the water to get her tied feet loose. She only partially sliced through the rope before having to come up, gasping for air. Taking another deep breath, she dove under again, and again before finally succeeding.

"We need to get out of this water now," Bree said. "You're shivering. Climb up to the bow. I'll be right behind you."

Patrizia went up the stairs with Bree following behind. The boat was tipped partially on its side, with the transom underwater and the bow sticking up in the air. They climbed up the walkaround, holding onto the rail as the rain pelted them. Patrizia reached the top first and clung with a white-knuckled grip, her arms trembling.

"Are you alright?" Bree asked, shouting over the wind, rain, and waves.

"Yes."

"I'm going back down to look for things we'll need. Be right back."

"Be careful."

Patrizia wanted to help, but felt too weak. It seemed ironic to her that after all these years of trying to protect Brianna, Brianna was now trying to protect her.

She watched Bree slowly climb back down, grasping the rail as the waves kept smacking her.

Bree waded over to the captain's chair. She shielded her face from the pouring rain as she took a look at the VHF radio mounted on the console in front of her. Her heart sank. Scott had rendered it useless. She pushed the button anyways. Nothing.

She went down the stairs and began to look through the cupboards for anything that might provide warmth, shield them from the rain, or help them survive this night.

Reaching up, she opened one cupboard and then another. Finally, she found something useful. A tarp. That would provide some relief, blocking them from the storm. On the shelf below it was a black canvas bag. She pulled it down to the counter, then unzipped it.

Bree, for the first time, felt hope. She pulled out a flashlight, flares, a first-aid kit, and. . .

Jackpot!

A handheld VHF radio! Tears of joy began to stream down her face as she stared unbelievingly at her find. She choked back the tears and stuffed everything back in the bag and zipped it up. Dragging it up the stairs with the tarp under her arm, the bag was the lightest heavy object she ever had to carry.

When she got to the top, she saw that Patrizia had been anxiously watching for her. Bree stopped and unzipped the bag, pulling out the radio. She held onto the rail with one hand and with a big, wide smile, she waved the radio in the air to show Patrizia what she had.

Patrizia clapped her hands together and began to laugh and cry.

Bree didn't go back up to her for fear of slipping while walking up the walkaround. The water rushing down made the deck slippery and she wasn't risking losing that radio for anything.

She sat down on the top step so the wall would block some of the rain and noise from the wind. Water washed around her and her hair was drenched and matted to her head.

She grabbed the flashlight, turned it on, and aimed it at the radio. She stared at it, not sure how it worked.

Seeing a red button marked "distress," she pushed it. Next, she held down the button on the side. Encouraged by the static she heard, she began shouting into the radio.

"Mayday! Mayday! Mayday!" she said, rapid-firing the words. "Coast Guard! Coast Guard! Coast Guard!"

Releasing the button, she waited and was quickly answered.

"This is the United States Coast Guard. Air Station Traverse City. What is your call sign and name? Over."

"Kinsley. That's all I know. We're on the Kinsley."

"What is your position? Over."

"I don't know! Umm. I can see the South Manitou Lighthouse. We're south of there."

"You are on the Kinsley, south of South Manitou Island. State your emergency. Over."

Bree screamed as the boat shifted in the sand, lurching more to one side. Losing her calm and forgetting protocol, she blurted out her response. "We're on a shoal! Help us! The back of the boat's under water and the bow's up in the air. I'm sitting in water right now. Hurry! The boat's busting up."

"How many people are on board and what is their condition? Over."

"Just two of us. We're okay, but Patrizia is shaking bad. Her lips are purple. Possible hypothermia? I don't know!"

"What is the description of your vessel? Over."

"It's a white cruiser." Bree looked around. "Sea Ray."

"There are two on board. One suffering hypothermia. White Sea Ray cruiser busting up and taking on water. We will send someone to help you. Put on your life jackets immediately. Over."

"We don't have any! They were thrown overboard."

"Your life jackets were thrown overboard? Over."

"Yes! We were taken against our will. When our boat crashed, they took the life raft and left us here. They threw the jackets over! Please hurry!"

"How many have left the boat? Over."

"Two. Two men. Louis and Scott."

"Can you switch your frequency and stay on the line? Over."

"No. I've got to get up on the bow to check on Patrizia. I'll need both hands to hold onto the rail and tarp."

"Can you switch to Channel 72 so we can track you?"

Bree looked and saw a dial marked 'channel.' "Yes. I think so."

"Help will be on the way. Over."

"Hurry."

"Affirmative. Over and out."

Bree put the radio back in the bag and took out items she didn't need. She stuffed the tarp in there and zipped it up. Carefully timing her movements between waves and holding onto the boat and bag, she made her climb up to Patrizia.

Patrizia was anxiously watching her. "Did you get through? Is help coming?"

"Yes," Bree said, sitting next to Patrizia. With trembling hands, she took out a light and attached it to the rail behind her. "They're going to send help. We've got to huddle together for warmth. I don't know how long it'll take them. I've got a tarp we can wrap around us." It sounded easy, but the wind repeatedly tried ripping the tarp out of their hands. The two of them struggled to hold onto it.

Communication was tough with all the noise, so they held onto the boat, tarp, and each other, shivering and silent.

Bree started to say something, but Patrizia had her eyes closed. No sound was coming out but her lips were moving. Bree waited. If her mother had some connections with the man upstairs, it certainly couldn't hurt their situation any.

A booming, cracking sound split the air, making them jump and scream. The lightning was too close. Crying, they held on tight to each other, realizing their first day together might very well be their last.

CHAPTER EIGHTEEN

The Nighthawk continued further out into the lake. "Do you know where they were headin'?" Frank asked.

"No," Denver answered, "but Louis asked me about the Manitou area. To avoid shoals, I think he'll head west of the islands and ride out the storm."

He searched the water in hope of seeing them, but visibility was minimal. All he could make out were raging waves and a darkening sky. Would they ever be able to find Bree, he wondered? He knew they were going as fast as they safely could, but it was taking forever to get anywhere.

The four of them rode along silently. Each time a wave precariously rocked the boat, Steven had to fight to keep from emptying his stomach.

After some time, Channel 16 crackled to life.

"Mayday. Mayday. Mayday."

Denver's heart raced as he heard Bree's voice. She was alive and able to call.

"That's Bree," Steven said. "We need to answer it."

Denver fought the urge to answer the call, hoping the Coast Guard would answer. The Coast Guard responded immediately.

Bree sounded scared, but calm, until she screamed. *What just happened?* A tide of awful scenarios flooded Denver's mind. The crew listened intently as Bree began to speak again. The boat had been hit hard by a wave and shifted, almost knocking Bree down the steps. She gave her location, a description of the boat's condition and who was with her. *Patrizia was with her? Bree's birth mom?*

It was too much.

After the call ended, Denver called the Coast Guard to offer assistance, giving his vessel name and coordinates. The Nighthawk, being in the best position to give aid, was approved to proceed.

Denver placed the speaker back. "Let me take the wheel."

Frank stepped to the side and Denver took over. To change course, he slowed and waited to be in the right position. Throwing the wheel hard over, he quickly applied power. The boat turned sharply and Steven's gut somersaulted. Unable to fight it anymore, he leaned over the railing to empty his stomach of its contents. He felt terrible and helpless.

Denver headed for the lighthouse, careful not to run aground. Soon they spotted the SOS beacon.

"There she is!" Charlie said.

"Holy shit," Frank said as they neared the Kinsley. "She's in bad shape."

Denver saw Bree and Patrizia waving their arms at them. "Frank," Denver said, fighting to keep control of his emotions. "I need you to take the wheel and keep her steady. We can't get too close to the shoal, so I'm going to throw a life ring over to Bree." Frank nodded and took over while Denver hooked a line to the life ring, getting it ready to throw to the stranded vessel.

Seeing what he was going to do, Bree got into position, as close to the boat's edge as she could, and held onto the rail, waiting.

Denver blew a whistle. "Rope!" he yelled, then heaved the ring. It sailed through the air. Bree stretched, reaching into the air as it came near. The wind toyed with it, keeping it just out of reach. As it dropped towards her, the boat moved slightly, throwing Bree off balance. As she began falling forward, Denver yelled. In hopelessness, he grabbed handfuls of his hair with both hands. "Nooooo!"

Patrizia grabbed Bree's shirt, yanking her backwards to safety.

In anguish, Denver dropped to the deck, sure—for a second—he had lost her. Pounding his fist on the deck, he stood up. He would not chance that happening again.

Putting on a life vest, he attached a line to it.

Frank shook his head, not liking the idea of putting one more person at risk, but he knew it was pointless to argue.

"When I'm ready, I'll give the signal," Denver said to Steven and Charlie. "Pull her in quickly. When Bree gets near the boat, signal Frank to put the boat in neutral. Speed is crucial. We have to have the propellers stopped and he'll have no steering. Haul her in fast so Frank can get the boat back into gear immediately."

Denver sat on the gunwale and swung his legs out over the water. Lightning streaked across the sky and the thunder cracked, heavy raindrops prickling against his skin. Denver took one last look above the island and could see why some had believed evil spirits lived there. The storm seemed to be centering the worst of its assault directly over the island, as if it harbored some personal vendetta against it. He had never seen nature unleash such wrath.

Dropping into the ice-cold water, he felt chilled, but the wet suit offered some insulation.

Charlie kept the searchlight on him and Frank steered. The first wave came and swallowed Denver up, but he sprang back to the surface. He was stroking and kicking, trying to make headway toward the Kinsley before the next wave. Charlie let the line out a little at a time so Denver wouldn't be slammed into the side of the grounded vessel. When close enough and in the trough of a wave, his feet touched on the shoal. He quickly made his move and grabbed onto the side rail of the Kinsley and wrapped his arms around it. Denver held on with all the strength he had as the next wave came. The force and power of the rushing water almost tore him away, but he held on. When the wave subsided, he pulled himself over the rail, taking a moment to regain his breath.

"Denver!" Bree said, her teeth chattering. She clung to him, sobbing.

"Thank you, God!" Patrizia said, relieved that help had arrived in time. Over the years, she sometimes wondered if God was even listening to her prayers. Not until recently had she realized just how many of her prayers He had answered. "Thank you, Jesus," she said in a whisper.

"We've got to get out of here now. This boat can't take much more," said Denver. "Bree, you go first."

"No. Patrizia's in bad shape. She needs to go first."

"No, Brianna, you go," Patrizia said.

"I'm with Bree on this one," Denver said as he took another look at Patrizia. She was shivering uncontrollably. "You're going first."

Denver took his life jacket off and helped Patrizia with it. Her fingers were shaking so badly that Denver had to fasten and tighten it. He grabbed a ladder and hooked it over the gunwale, then attached the line to Patrizia's life jacket. After helping her down the ladder and slowly into the water, he gave the signal.

Charlie and Steven worked together to pull her in as quickly as possible.

"Get down in the cabin," Charlie said to Patrizia. "There are dry blankets inside there."

"But Brianna..."

"I can help her better if I'm not worrying about you."

Patrizia obeyed and stepped down on shaky legs. She fell and had to pull herself up. She found the blankets and curled up in them. As she slowly warmed up, it felt like thousands of little needles were pricking at her body.

Up on deck Charlie threw the life preserver and line back to the Kinsley. Denver ducked out of the way and grabbed for it when it hit the deck. "You're next," he said.

Bree clung tightly to him. "I love you, Denver."

"I love you too," he answered. Quickly, he helped her get the life preserver on and hooked the line to it before giving her a kiss. "Be careful."

"You too," she said, and climbed over the rail into the water. Charlie and Steven pulled her in.

Frank had his hands full trying to control the boat against the fury of the storm.

"Steven!" Bree said, surprised to see him there.

"Bree, I'm so glad you're alright. I was so worried!" he said, giving her a hug.

"Go down below with Patrizia and get in some blankets. You need to get warmed up," Charlie said, interrupting.

"No, I'm waiting for Denver."

Charlie didn't bother to argue. He knew Bree well enough to know it wouldn't do any good. He wrapped up the line and gave it and the preserver a heave. It fell short of the Kinsley.

"Can you get closer?" Charlie yelled up at Frank.

"I'll try!"

Charlie threw it again and almost made it. Denver reached to grab it and missed as a wave washed over the deck. Thrown off balance, Denver slipped and was swept overboard.

"Denver!" Bree yelled, running over to the rail. "Charlie! I don't see him!"

"We'll find him." He slowly turned the searchlight to cover as much area as possible and improve his visibility range. Bree waited frantically as Charlie scanned the water's surface, repeatedly. Finally, he turned it off.

"What are you doing? We can't give up!" Bree said, giving him an angry shove. "We're not leaving him!"

"Bree. We don't have a choice. We can't get in any closer. He'll go for shore and it's not far. His wet suit will give him some buoyancy and insulation from the cold. We have a better chance of finding him from shore."

"No," she said weakly, shaking her head.

Steven put his arm around her. "Charlie's right, Bree. Frank will get us to the bay and we'll find him. For now, you can check on Patrizia."

Bree had forgotten about her. Slowly, she made her way inside the cabin.

"What is wrong?" Patrizia asked. "Where is Denver?"

Bree shook her head and turned away, wiping at her tears. "He fell overboard."

Patrizia gasped. "They could not help him?"

"We're going to the island to look for him." Not wanting to discuss it, she began searching in the cupboards. "You need to eat something."

Finding crackers, she gave them to her. "This should be easy to keep down." Bree grabbed a blanket and sat next to Patrizia.

"I am so sorry about Denver. I pray that he will be all right."

Bree collapsed against her and began to sob.

"We will find him," Patrizia whispered as she put her arm around her. "We will find him."

Up on deck, Charlie called over the radio on Channel 16. "Mayday. Mayday. Mayday...this is the Nighthawk.... South of South Manitou Island...we have a man overboard and two females suffering from exhaustion and possible hypothermia. Need rescue assistance for man in water—unable to locate him.... We're heading for East Bay on South Manitou Island..."

The United States Coast Guard responded that a rescue helicopter was already deployed to the area and would commence search for the man overboard.

Frank steered the Nighthawk into East Bay and docked the boat.

"The four of you stay here," Charlie said. "Scott and Louis are out there somewhere. You'll be safe on the boat. If you see Scott or Louis heading towards the boat, push off and get away from the dock. I'll take the portable radio. If you need help, radio me."

"I want to..." Bree started to say.

"Damn it, Bree, NO!" Charlie said. "I know you're wanting to look for Denver, but it's not safe. I promise I'll do all I can to find him."

Bree nodded and sat back down, knowing Charlie was in no mood to argue. After he left, she sat impatiently for a while, but eventually couldn't take it anymore. She climbed over the side of the Nighthawk onto the dock.

"Bree! Where are you going?" Steven yelled. "You heard Charlie. Louis and Scott could be out there. Get back in the boat!"

"I can't!" Bree hollered and disappeared into the darkness.

"I'll try to get her to come back," Steven said, climbing over the side.

Frank shook his head. His only choices were to go after Bree and Steven or stay with Patrizia. Patrizia seemed to be doing a little better, but she was still shivering and weak. The only real option was to stay with her.

Bree ran down the shoreline calling out Denver's name. She desperately scanned the waters and occasionally looked up and down the storm-wracked strand, hoping to see him standing there. She went past the lighthouse where she thought the Kinsley had been. She stood in the rain looking out at the water. Did she see something out there, or was it wishful thinking? After staring for a long time, she decided it was her imagination. She walked further down the beach and then headed back.

"Where are you, Denver!" she cried out and plopped down on the beach. Cold and tired, she pulled her knees up to her chest for warmth and wrapped her arms around them. Bree rested her head on her knees. When she looked up again she saw him.

"Denver," she whispered to herself, almost afraid to believe what she was seeing.

Jumping up, she ran to him. Denver was trying to stand, but a wave knocked him back down and pushed him a few feet closer to shore. Slowly, he got up on his feet. The wet suit he was wearing had given him some protection, but he still felt shaky and exhausted. When knocked off the boat, he'd reached out, hoping to grab hold of the railing. Instead he grabbed the ladder and it was ripped from the boat's side. Being made of floatable plastic, he clung to it, using it as a makeshift raft. He paddled when he could, and when a wave swallowed him up had hung on until he surfaced again.

"Denver!" Bree said, now in a full run.

"Bree," he answered back, starting to smile.

He waited on rubbery legs for her to reach him. When Bree was a couple feet away, a sudden loud cracking sound split the air. At first, he thought it was thunder.

Bree's eyes turned wide and frozen as she was thrust forward toward Denver.

"Bree?" he said as he grabbed her, confused.

She slumped down in his arms. When he looked at his hand, it was covered in blood. "Bree!" he yelled louder. Panic swept through him. He saw the hole in Bree's shirt at the back of her right shoulder. Blood was spurting out. Looking up, he saw Louis striding past the lighthouse with a gun in his hand. He was headed towards them.

Unsure of what to do and unable to run or hide, Denver moved Bree away from the water's edge, lowering her to the ground. To shield Bree from Louis, he laid on top of her. His mind raced. Seeing his grandmother's worried face, he whispered, "I'm sorry, Grandmother. You were right." His body tensed and he closed his eyes as he waited for the gunshot. Time froze in eternity.

He kept waiting, but the shot didn't come. Instead, he heard an eerie shrieking sound that started low and rose in pitch. It was filled with an intense fury. He had never heard anything like it before. He looked up, afraid of what demons he might see.

Patrizia was standing behind Louis, with her arms stretched over her head and her face twisted with rage. The wind was whipping her hair wildly around her head. Lightning flashed across the sky, illuminating and intensifying the image that would be etched in Denver's mind forever. She continued to shriek as she brought the boulder in her hands crushing down on Louis's skull, a fatal blow.

Louis crumpled to the ground. Slowly. To Denver, all motion seemed to be laden with lead.

Charlie and Steven heard the gunshot and came running. Frank showed up, not too far behind them.

When they got there, they saw Patrizia pounding on Louis with her fists. She was shouting angry words in Italian, words that Charlie assumed he was lucky he couldn't understand. He grabbed Patrizia around the waist and gently but firmly pulled her off. She was still shouting and sobbing, shaking her fist at Louis. Slowly, she calmed as the energy drained from her. Charlie sat her down on the ground. He kept one arm around her, and with his other hand lifted Louis's wrist to feel for a pulse. He set it back down. "You won't have to worry about that sonofabitch ever again."

Patrizia sat there, staring at the dead body, waiting to feel something, anything, but she felt nothing. All the anger and fear that was bottled up inside her had exploded and disintegrated. Drained, she lost track of time, but when she looked up everyone was gathered around Bree.

"Brianna," she said to herself, snapping back into reality. She got up and stumbled over to them.

Denver had Bree's head resting in his lap. He was trying to keep her upper body, where the bullet had entered, elevated. "I need something to wrap around this wound!" he said. Charlie took off his shirt and T-shirt, tearing them into strips that Denver wrapped over Bree's shoulder and down around her side.

Denver kept pressure applied to the wound while Charlie called the Coast Guard on the radio.

Denver could hear parts of what he was saying. "Abort search for man overboard.... Need transport on South Manitou Island near the lighthouse...one gunshot victim—critical condition, one dead, two suffering from exhaustion and possible hypothermia.... I'm Charles Miller, a police officer with the Frankfort Police Department. I'm off-duty and carrying a concealed weapon."

It just didn't seem real. Denver looked at the shirts he had wrapped around the wound. They were already soaked through. Somehow, the bleeding had to slow or stop completely. "Steven! Frank! Run to the Nighthawk. Get the insulated blanket and whatever else you can find!"

They took off running and returned promptly.

"Hang in there, Bree. Help is on the way," Denver said in a quiet voice, trying to keep Bree relaxed as he wrapped the blanket around her. Charlie took a coat they had brought back and helped Patrizia put it on.

Bree tried, but failed, to say something to Denver. It was getting harder and harder to keep her eyes open. Denver could see she was getting weaker. "Don't give up on me, Bree. Don't go to sleep." She tried to fight it, but she was slipping in and out of consciousness.

"Where are they?" Denver shouted.

As if in answer, the rescue helicopter came into view.

Charlie grabbed his flashlight, jumped up, and ran, shining the light on the ground to aid in being located.

The helicopter, an HH-65 Dolphin, hovered above. As a searchlight shined on the ground, a flight mechanic appeared in the doorway. Quickly, the rescue swimmer was deployed, rappelling downward.

Charlie motioned him over to where Bree was lying. He checked her vitals. When the Stokes litter came down, the swimmer grabbed it. Together they carefully moved Bree into the basket; the swimmer secured her and gave the signal for her to be hoisted up. While she was being lifted, he quickly went over to check Louis's pulse.

"We're leaving him here. There's nothing we can do for him," he said to Charlie. "We can't spare a minute."

When the basket came back down, the swimmer got Patrizia strapped in to be hoisted up. She was still trembling uncontrollably. "Bree's gonna make it," Charlie said to her. "She's in good hands now."

While the swimmer was busy, Charlie walked over to Denver. "Are you wanting to go with them?"

"Yes. Someone has to be there with Bree."

"You're shivering and exhausted, so this shouldn't be hard to do—look a little sicker or they might not take you. Me and Steven will come up to the hospital as soon as possible."

"Alright. Thanks."

The Coast Guard operated quickly and efficiently. Soon the helicopter was out of sight with its three rescue victims, on its way to Munson Healthcare in Traverse City.

Charlie had volunteered and obtained permission to bring Louis's body to Frankfort. Having contacted his sergeant, it was arranged that a transport for the body would be waiting there for him. Charlie, Steven, and Frank grabbed Louis and carried him unceremoniously to the Nighthawk. The storm was subsiding and traveling east over the mainland. Frank figured it was safe to head back.

When aboard the Nighthawk and on their way, Steven made the call he had been dreading. Telling Mom and Dad what had happened wouldn't be easy.

A TIME TO HEAL

CHAPTER NINETEEN

At the hospital, they took Bree in immediately to assess her condition. Denver filled out the admission papers and gave them as much information as he could. He called Bree's parents and asked Betty the medical history questions on the sheet. It was a long drive for them, so it would be a few hours before they arrived. He also called his parents and asked them to explain to Grandmother everything that had happened.

Alone, he sat in the emergency waiting room. Even though they had examined and released him, they let Denver stay in the hospital pants and gown until Charlie arrived with clothes for him.

Every second he sat waiting was torture. Getting up, he went to check on Patrizia. She was hooked to an IV and lying on a hospital bed. "How are you doing?"

"I am fine. How are you?"

"Alright, I guess. I'll be a lot better when I know how Bree is doing."

"You don't know how she is either? I have heard nothing."

"I'm waiting for the doctor to come talk to us. They told me he would."

"I hope it is soon. I do not know if I can take much more waiting."

As she finished speaking, the doctor came through the door and introduced himself. He wasted no time getting to the point. "Brianna has lost a large amount of blood. Our main objective right now is to get her stable, so we are administering blood. Luckily, the bullet missed all major organs. It did, however, cause a lot of trauma to the shoulder, including bone and tissue damage, which resulted in excessive bleeding. We can't operate to remove the bullet until her condition improves. It's a good thing she arrived here when she did. She is still in critical condition and the next seventy-two hours will be very important. The outlook is favorable, but I can't make any promises. Does anyone have any questions?"

"Can we see her now?" Denver asked.

"Only for a few minutes. She needs her rest."

A nurse came and helped Patrizia into a wheelchair, and Denver pushed her and her IV down to Bree's room. Bree looked as pale as the sheets she was lying on; her eyes were closed, and she was in a deep sleep. She had an IV and monitors hooked up to her. A nurse came in and checked her oxygen and IV. She smiled and reminded them not to stay too long.

Denver took Bree's hand in his. "Bree, if you can hear me, this is Denver. You're at the hospital. You're going to be okay. Patrizia is here. Hang in there. You're going to be okay." He hesitated, trying to pull himself together. Unable to speak anymore, he stepped to the side while swiping away tears. He then maneuvered Patrizia next to Bree's bedside.

"Brianna," she said softly, gently holding Bree's hand and affectionately fussing with her hair. She looked so frail and small, just like when she was her little girl. "My sweet, sweet Brianna. I love you, my darling."

She hesitated for a moment before singing softly to Bree, first in English, the lullaby she always sang to her when she was little:

Go to sleep, go to sleepy
In the arms of your mother.
Go to sleep, lovely child.
Go to sleepy, child so lovely,
Go to sleep, go to sleepy
In the arms of your mother.

Fa la ninna, fa la nanna
Nella braccia della mamma
Fa la ninna bel bambina,
Fa la nanna bambina bel.
Fa la ninna, fa la nanna
Nella braccia della mamma.

When finished, she squeezed and patted Bree's hand. Faintly, Bree's hand moved, as if trying to give a squeeze back.

"Look!" Patrizia said to Denver. "Her hand!"

Denver looked over her shoulder and saw Bree's hand slightly moving.

"Do you think she heard me?"

"Yes, yes I do." They both began sobbing tears of joy.

"Bree, we're here for you," Denver said. "I love you, Bree. You're at Munson Hospital in Traverse City. Your parents and Steven are on their way."

There was no more response, but Patrizia and Denver were hopeful and believed she heard everything.

They waited there silently, until a nurse came and motioned for them to leave. "She needs her rest."

Denver wheeled Patrizia back to her room and the nurse helped her back into bed. They didn't have to wait very long for the doctor.

"How are you feeling?" he asked.

"Fine. Tired, but fine."

"That's to be expected under the circumstances. You've been through a lot. Luckily your case of hypothermia was mild. Your shivering has ceased and your core temperature is back where it should be. Everything looks good. I see no reason why I can't release you. Just take it easy for a few days and make sure you get something to eat. You need to get your strength back up. Are there any questions?"

"No."

"The nurse will be in to get you checked out."

Soon after Patrizia finished the discharge procedure, Steven arrived, Charlie following shortly after.

"I bought both of you sweats and a T-shirt. Hopefully I guessed the right sizes. I'm not much of a hand at fashion, but it sure beats the get-ups you two have on."

"What?" Denver asked. "You don't like these? They're all the rage here."

"I see that," said Charlie. "How's Bree doing?"

Denver brought Steven and Charlie up to date, and Steven went down the hallway to call his parents with the current information—or at least parts of it. Not wanting them to panic on the drive up, he downplayed the seriousness of what had happened and left certain things out. They could be filled in when they arrived.

"It is all my fault that this happened," Patrizia said.

"How can you say that?" Denver asked. "You saved her life—a couple of times. Louis would have shot both of us if you hadn't stopped him."

"Louis wanted to hurt me. He used Brianna to do it. It should be me in there, not her. She does not deserve any of this."

"Neither do you," Charlie said. "Louis pulled the trigger, not you." He tried to lighten things up a bit by changing the conversation. "I was pretty impressed. In your weak and frail condition, you were able to lift that boulder over your head. You looked like Hercules. I know I won't be trying to push *you* around."

Patrizia laughed and cried at the same time. "It was adrelin," she said.

Charlie looked confused for a second. "Adrenaline," he said, when he figured out what she had meant to say. She nodded affirmation.

"You both need rest and something to eat. There's no easy way of saying this: You both look like hell."

"Nice. Charlie always knows the right thing to say," Denver explained to Patrizia.

"Seriously, you both have been through a lot physically and emotionally."

Charlie walked over to the receptionist. "Care if I borrow this?" he asked, and brought over a wheelchair. "I'm at least taking you to get something to eat. We're going to the cafeteria."

"I do not need a wheelchair," Patrizia protested. "I can walk."

"It's a long walk to the cafeteria and you need your strength. Don't argue with me, just get in. Your chariot awaits."

Patrizia reluctantly got in.

"What about you? Are you coming, Denver?"

"No, I want to stay in the waiting room in case I hear anything. Could you two bring me something back? I *am* starting to get hungry."

"Sure can," Charlie said, making some engine and shifting noises as he took off.

Patrizia was laughing and hiding her face. "This is embarrassing. You are crazy!" People were looking at them as they rounded the corner and Charlie made squealing sounds. He wheeled her over to a table.

"Tell me what you like and I shall get it for you," Charlie said in a servant-like manner.

"Please," she answered, playing the role. "I am famished. A little of everything, and make it snappy!"

"Be careful what you ask for," he said, and came back with a plate piled high.

"I cannot eat all of this!" she said, not believing how full the plate was.

"Try. I think you can."

Patrizia started eating, reluctantly at first, but with greater gusto as she began realizing how hungry she was. She ate with a hearty appetite and devoured all of it. Charlie watched her finish the last bite.

"I cannot believe I ate that much. Are you still impressed with me?" she challenged.

"Yes," he said, being serious for once. "I believe that I am."

CHAPTER TWENTY

Charlie wheeled Patrizia back to the waiting room where Denver was waiting. He left to fill out a report at the police station, and then went home. This was a time for family. He would check in again tomorrow to see how Bree was doing.

Denver and Patrizia sat next to each other on the couch, while Steven paced the floor.

"Maybe you should lie down and try to get some sleep," Denver suggested to Patrizia.

"I cannot sleep."

"If you can't sleep, we might as well talk. We're going to be here a long time. Maybe we can get to know each other better. If it's none of my business, just say so, but what the hell was all of this about? After seeing what Louis was capable of, I can understand why you gave Bree up. I assume you were trying to protect her, but what was the deal with Louis? How did you get mixed up with a guy like that?"

"It is painful to talk about, but you have been good to my Brianna. You even risked your life to save her. For this reason, I do not mind sharing everything with you. I know you have her best interest in your heart."

Patrizia told him everything, starting with her days in school up until the present. Denver listened silently. When she finished, he put his arm around her and she leaned against him.

"Your life has been hell, but you don't have to worry anymore. Louis is gone. You'll never have to look over your shoulder again."

Patrizia nodded as she closed her eyes and drifted off to sleep.

Denver sat still so she wouldn't wake up. The next hour passed slowly and left him too much time to think. He'd come so close to losing Bree, and she wasn't out of danger yet.

Denver saw Tom and Betty when they arrived. They walked over to the nurse's station and were told it would be a moment before they could see Bree. Steven walked over to them and gave them both a hug, then began filling them in on the details he had been dreading to tell them.

"Shot?" Tom asked, incredulously. "I thought you said she was in a boating accident."

"I did, and that part is true," Steven said. "I didn't want to tell you everything on the phone. I knew you had a long drive up and knowing Bree was in the hospital would be enough to worry about."

"Why would anyone want to shoot Bree? What happened?" Tom asked, trying to reign in his emotions.

"It turns out that Louis wasn't the wonderful dad he was pretending to be."

While Steven was talking, Denver had carefully freed himself from Patrizia and laid her down on the couch. He walked over to Tom and Betty and said hello.

"Hello, Denver," Betty answered as she gave him a hug. "I can't believe any of this is happening. It—it doesn't seem real."

"Steven just told us Bree was shot," Tom cut in, impatiently getting right to the point. "Why the hell would anyone want to shoot Bree?"

Denver took a deep breath. He knew Tom was wanting answers and dragging it out would only make him angrier. There was no way to make this easy.

"It turns out that Louis isn't Bree's birth father, even though he was listed on the birth certificate as the father. He's also—or at least he was—a higher-up in the Mafia."

"The Mafia!" Tom shouted in disbelief.

"Yes. Patrizia took Bree and left him years ago to protect them from his abuse and way of life. Louis recently got out of prison and came looking for them. He abducted both of them and held them against their will on a boat. I'll fill you in on all the other details later, but they ended up on South Manitou Island, where Louis shot Bree. She's lucky to be alive."

The commotion and raised voices woke Patrizia up. She got up off the couch and started walking towards the group. Even though they had changed, she still recognized them: Tom's hair had grayed some, and Betty now wore glasses and had short, permed hair.

Tom and Betty saw her coming towards them and stared in disbelief. They knew instantly she was the woman in the picture Bree had shown them.

"Patrizia," Denver said, "I would like you to meet Bree's parents, Tom and Betty. Tom and Betty, this is Patrizia, Bree's birth mother."

There was a moment of awkward silence before they exchanged greetings. They went over to the chairs in the lobby and sat down. To spare Patrizia from having to go through it again, Denver gave them a brief, condensed version of Patrizia's life and filled in some of the events of the last twenty-four hours.

A nurse walked over to them. "Brianna is awake now. She is still weak, so the visits must be short. She's been asking to see her mom, dad, Steven, and Denver. Only two at a time, please."

Denver motioned for Tom and Betty to go in. Steven snuck in with them. Patrizia tried to hide it, but Denver caught a glimpse of the hurt in her eyes.

"Patrizia," Denver said. "I know Bree. She won't hold any of this against you. Just give her time. It's natural for her to first want the ones that raised her. They were the ones she went to whenever she was hurt or scared. Bree's a very understanding person. She won't judge you for the decisions you had to make."

"I am grateful that they have been so good to Brianna. It was what I always hoped and prayed for, but I cannot help but feel a little envious. It should have been me that raised her. There is nobody to blame except Louis. He has caused so much pain."

When Tom, Betty, and Steven came out, the relief they felt was obvious. They were relaxed, even laughing and smiling.

"She wants to see you now, Denver," Betty said. She then turned to Patrizia, who was sitting quietly on a chair. "She wants to see you too, Patrizia."

"She does?" she asked. They nodded confirmation.

Patrizia quickly rose to her feet. She was apprehensive—not knowing what Bree wanted to tell her. But at least she would be able to see her, maybe make her understand why she'd done what she had. Knowing that Brianna was safe from Louis was enough to make her feel a little better. Maybe she should've felt guilty for what she'd done on the island, but she didn't.

Denver and Patrizia walked down to Bree's room. Denver went over to Bree first. He gave her a cautious hug and a quick kiss.

"Hi," he said. "How are you doing?"

"Fine," she answered, smiling at him.

"You sure had me scared for a while."

"You had me scared too," she answered. She reached for his hand and gave it a squeeze. She had so much she wanted to say, but was too tired. It would have to wait.

Bree looked past Denver to Patrizia. "You look a lot better than the last time I saw you."

Patrizia stepped forward. "I feel fine. It is you that I have been worried about."

"I'm tired, but other than that I feel okay. I suppose I'll be hurting when they take me off these painkillers." She rested a second, then continued, "I talked to Mom and Dad. They said it was okay if I had a second mom. Do you care if I call you Mom?"

She nodded her head enthusiastically. Denver handed Patrizia a box of tissues and she shared it with Bree.

"Women," Denver said, shaking his head as he turned and walked to the foot of the bed. It gave him time to wipe away his tears without them seeing.

Early in the morning the surgery was done to remove the bullet. Everything went as they had hoped. After they were sure Bree would be fine, Patrizia and Denver left the hospital to get some sleep. The recent events had taken a toll on them. Tom, Betty, and Steven stayed until they came back later that evening, then they left to get some rest.

Charlie stopped in to see Bree while Denver and Patrizia were there. He brought balloons tied to a box of chocolates. As usual, he had everyone laughing and in good spirits. Even though Bree was enjoying his company, something was bothering her.

"Have they found Scott yet?" she asked.

Charlie slowly smiled. "They sure did. Found him the next day on the north side of the island." He was starting to chuckle now. "The fool decided to hike through the woods instead of staying on the trails and picked himself up a little souvenir."

"No," Denver said, joining in on the laughter. "He didn't."

"Oh, he sure did." The two were laughing at their own private joke.

"What's so funny?" Bree asked, getting irritated. "What happened?"

"The boy got into some poison ivy. When they got to him, he was covered with red patches from head to toe—itching like crazy. You know they hated to do it, but they had to put handcuffs on him. On the boat ride to Frankfort and the ride in the patrol car to the station, I was told he was squirming around like a virgin bride on her wedding night."

Denver and Charlie chuckled as they thought of poor Scott.

"I can't say that I feel sorry for him," Bree said, starting to relax as Charlie continued his story. Knowing they had found Scott made her feel better.

After Charlie left, the room became quiet and Bree seemed to be feeling more on edge again. She tried to be pleasant, but it didn't last long. She couldn't get comfortable. The food was lousy. Nothing pleased her.

"What's wrong, Bree?" Denver finally asked.

"What's wrong?" she repeated. "What's wrong? Let me think. I trusted him! I trusted him and he left me on the boat to die! The whole time he pretended to be my father. He pretended to love me, and at the same time he was planning to sell me to some low-lives like I was merchandise! How can you ask what's wrong? He was so charming and so sincere, or was I just plain stupid? I fell for the whole damn thing!"

She was biting her lower lip, her pillow hugged in a vise-like grip. Denver was stunned. He didn't know what to say. He understood the anger. He was feeling some of that himself, but he didn't like being the target.

There was fire in Bree's eyes, but when she saw the hurt expression on Denver's face she felt ashamed.

"What is wrong with me? I'm so sorry, Denver. You're the last person I want to hurt, and I'm taking everything out on you." She began to sob into her pillow.

"I think with all you've been through, you're entitled to an emotional outburst." He gently pulled the pillow away from her face and sat on the edge of the bed. "I love you, Bree. It will take more than that to drive me away." He gently wiped the tears from her cheek and brushed her hair back out of her eyes.

Patrizia had been standing in the corner of the room. Denver and Bree were looking at each other, communicating without saying a word. Patrizia slipped out the door to leave them alone. She understood exactly how Bree was feeling. The same man had deceived her a long time ago.

The next day, Bree was in better spirits. She was told she might be able to go home in a couple days. When Denver came in he had a visitor with him.

"Grandmother! It's so good to see you," said Bree. "I was worried about you."

"I am fine. For long walks, I need my companion now," she said, referring to the walker she was holding onto. "But I am doing well. I had to see for myself that you were doing as well as they said. Denver has been pacing the floor like a lost puppy, so I wasn't sure."

"Grandmother!" Denver said, giving her a look.

"Well, it's true."

Bree laughed. She loved watching them tease each other.

"Are you sure you're feeling okay?" Bree asked. "I was on my way to see you when..." she hesitated for a moment. "Let's just say I got sidetracked."

Grandmother patted her hand. "You are a strong girl. You will get through all of this."

"Thank you. With all the support I have, I think you're right." She looked around her room at all the plants and cards. Denver must have told his family about her love for plants.

"Grandmother," Denver asked. "Is it all right if I leave you here to visit with Bree for a while? I have an errand I have to run."

"That will be fine. I still have more stories about you to tell."

Bree and Grandmother laughed. Denver just rolled his eyes and moaned.

"Is there anything you need, Bree?" he asked.

She shook her head no, so he said his goodbyes and left.

Bree looked at Grandmother for a moment. "You knew all along, didn't you? It wasn't just me in danger. Denver was in danger too. As close as you two are, I'm surprised you didn't try to get him to stay away from me."

Grandmother had a sheepish look on her face.

"I will be honest with you, Bree. At first, I did try to convince Denver to forget about you. You would bring him trouble. I even thought about talking to you about it."

"What made you change your mind?"

"It didn't take long for me to realize it would not do any good. You walked in his soul."

Bree smiled.

"He did not know it at that time. Men are always the last to know." Grandmother leaned forward. "Some things never change."

"You should have told me," Bree said. "If I had known he was in danger I would have stayed away from him."

"Denver would have been upset with me if I had. Everyone must choose their own path, Bree, wherever it may take them. We can only hope and pray for the best."

They continued their conversation until Denver came back. He stood quietly behind Grandmother, but soon became fidgety.

Grandmother sensed he had something on his mind. "I have had enough," she finally said, slowly getting up from her chair. "I'm getting nervous having you hover over me like that. I will wait for you down in the lobby." She told Bree goodbye and shuffled out the door and down the hallway.

Denver came over and sat on the edge of Bree's bed, taking her hand in his.

"Bree," he began. "I've had a lot of time to think these last few days. When I heard that Scott had you out on the Kinsley, I felt like my entire world was falling apart. I couldn't stand the thought of someone hurting you, or of losing you."

Bree started to speak, but Denver stopped her. "I have something I have to say to you. Please, let me finish." He gave her hand a squeeze and continued. "If I had any doubts before about how I felt about you, I don't now. You are in my thoughts every moment. You are the one I want to spend the rest of my life with. If you need more time to think about it, I understand, but I don't need any more time to know what I want." He pulled out a small box that he'd had tucked in his pocket. "Bree, will you marry me?"

Bree was speechless. She stared at him, not knowing what to say. She knew she had never felt about anyone the way she felt about Denver, but they had only been a couple for a few months. They'd never really discussed any formal commitment at all; it just seemed to evolve naturally into a relationship where they saw only each other.

She took the small box and opened it. Inside was a diamond ring. It was beautiful. Tears came to her eyes. She looked at Denver. Sheila had been right. He had eyes you could drown in. He was looking at her so intensely that it made her smile. Knowing she meant so much to him made her feel warm inside.

Just as she was about to answer, Patrizia and the Darbys walked into the room together. They were laughing and in good spirits.

"So, how is our girl today?" Tom asked.

"Fine," Bree answered, but she was still looking at Denver.

"She should be fine," Steven said. "Look at all the cards, plants, and gifts she's been getting. Bree will do anything for attention."

Normally, that kind of comment would've sparked a response from Bree, but her mind seemed to be lost somewhere else.

"Did we interrupt something?" Betty asked, sensing that maybe their timing was not so good.

"Yes," Bree said, smiling and nodding her head.

Betty looked back and forth between Denver and Bree. Something was definitely going on. "What?"

"Yes, I will marry you," she said to Denver.

He breathed a sigh of relief as he got up and gave her a hug and a kiss. Bree noticed that his hands were shaking as he slipped the ring on her finger.

The room was dead silent, but only for a few seconds.

Soon everything was in an uproar, with everyone laughing, hugging, and crying. Even some of the nurses stepped in to see what was going on.

The news would spread fast. The story about the little girl who was abandoned twenty years ago had become the talk of the town. Everyone was rooting for Bree to get better, and for the mom that had come back to save her. The wedding proposal would be well-received news.

Overwhelmed by it all, Patrizia snuck out of the room. "Thank you, Lord," she said silently. "Thank you."

SPECIAL THANKS

I did a lot of research for this story, but I also wanted to get personal experiences from people who have been out on Lake Michigan in a storm so I could get a feel for what it would be like. The following people were kind enough to let me interview them, and they shared their stories and knowledge about boating on Lake Michigan, rescues, and/or first aid: Robert Eastman, Janice Groulx, Dan Richards, John Sarya, Denny and Judy Rush.

I'd also like to thank my family and friends who have supported me; especially Debi. She taught me how to post pictures on my blog (michiganmary.com) and helped with all my technical difficulties – and there were a few. Most of all, she was as excited as I was about seeing my dream of being published come true. A friendship like that is priceless. Thank you Deb!

Last, but definitely not least, I'd like to thank Denver Doxtator for letting me use his name. It was perfect!